The
FALSE
RIDER

The
FALSE
RIDER

Max Brand

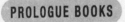
F+W Media, Inc.

Published by
PROLOGUE BOOKS
an imprint of F+W Media, Inc.
10151 Carver Road, Suite 200, Blue Ash, Ohio 45242
www.prologuebooks.com

ISBN 10: 1-4405-4934-6
ISBN 13: 978-1-4405-4934-2
eISBN 10: 1-4405-4932-X
eISBN 13: 978-1-4405-4932-8

Printed in the United States of America.

10 9 8 7 6 5 4 3 2 1

This book is available at quantity discounts for bulk purchases.
For information, please call 1-800-289-0963.

Contents

CHAPTER 1

Duff Gregor

Duff Gregor left the town of Piute on the run. It was not the first town which he had left with speed. In fact, he knew all about ways of leaving towns. He had left on foot, on horseback, in the blind baggage, and riding the rods. He had left a Mexican town, one day, tied face down on a wild horse; Mexicans are sure to serve up novelties. He had left more than one town riding a rail, and on two occasions wearing a coat of tar and feathers. The exit from Piute, as a matter of fact, had been rather a lucky one.

The reason lay in a card game. Most of Gregor's ups and downs in life sprang from cards.

This time he had just cut in a cold pack of his own in an interesting little game when the jack pot was piled high in the center of the table. And then a man drew a gun.

Gregor knew what the glare in the eyes and the sudden hunching of the shoulders meant. He was prepared out of the stores of old experience for just such gestures and attitudes, and for that reason he carried deep in a coat pocket a little two-barreled pistol, one of those silly, old-fashioned affairs that have the barrels built one on top of the other. It was a very short gun. At twenty paces it shot wild and hardly with force enough to break bones. But it looked no bigger than a tobacco pouch, say, and it threw a big slug. At a distance no greater than the width of a table it did real execution.

In this case its bullet sent the fellow who had reached for a gun toppling back out of his chair with a scream of agony. Duff Gregor was no fool with a gun. He had shot straight under the table with the first bullet. With the second, his hand now raised, he hit the light that hung from the ceiling in the back room of that hotel, and in the dark confusion that followed, he scraped the stakes off the table, kicked open a door, and got to a horse reasonably ahead of the other men in the card game.

He was not entirely ahead of their bullets, however, and when he was five miles out of Piute, that poor mustang began to fail and falter. When Gregor dismounted to look for causes, he discovered that the poor game animal had run all that distance hard and true while the life-blood was leaking out of it through a bullet wound.

Gregor was interested, but not touched. He cursed that pony for playing out on him, stripped off saddle and bridle, and did not waste an extra bullet to put the lost mustang out of its last agonies. Duff Gregor was a practical man, and he hated wasted gestures of sentimentality.

He was sufficiently practical, however, to know the value of carrying the saddle, the bridle, and the forty-foot hempen rope, for on the range he might come across another horse, and if he did, he would not stop to ask who owned it. He was not at all foolishly particular about such matters.

A range saddle is a heavy burden. A range bridle is not a light weight, and even forty feet of rope weighs something. But Duff Gregor turned himself into a plodding pack animal and endured his labor patiently. He had qualities, Duff Gregor, and the ability to make the best of a bad moment was one of them.

What he wanted most of all was to get distance between himself and Piute. He wanted the blue of a certain mountain range to the west between him and the thought of the angry citizens of that town, but he was well into the foothills before he saw a horse at hand.

He climbed a hill, looked down into a little valley where there was wood, water, and plenty of grass, and in the middle of that place he saw a chestnut stallion that looked able to jump over the moon if he heard so much as a whisper in the tall grass. He was shining like metal, that stallion. The westering sun made the gold of him burn.

Duff Gregor worked his way around until he was directly down-wind from the horse, and stalked with care for a full hot hour. When he came closer, he raised his head near the tops of the high grass and made out that there was no sweaty mark of bridle strap or saddle blanket on the horse; neither was there a saddle gall to patch with white the smooth gold of the stallion's back.

A wild horse? Well, if that was the case, Duff Gregor would find himself hitched to a comet, perhaps. But he had plenty of nerve. He had an extra share of courage that might have been dished out to make a sufficient portion for three ordinary men.

He had left the saddle and bridle, as meaningless encumbrances, farther up the hill. Now he went on, stealthily, making a noose in the rope. He was very close before the snort of the stallion warned him that his approach might have been discovered. Then, peering cautiously through the higher heads of the grass, he made out the golden stallion on guard, with head and tail high, and the look of a creature capable of bounding into the air and taking wing above the mountains at any moment.

Gregor rose out of that grass with a beautiful underhand cast of the rope, a trick that he had learned in Mexico in the old days. The noose settled fair and true around the neck of the big horse as he turned.

But he was a wild horse, apparently. The burn of the rope as he pulled taut had not stopped the stallion. Instead, he went off as fast as he could leg it with seventeen hands of muscle and bone. In the very end of the rope a snarl hooked around the leg of Gregor, who was snaked off his feet and skidded away through the grass with such speed that the blades stung his hands and face.

Unless he killed that stallion, he would be dragged to death. He got hold of his gun just as he was dragged through a patch of brush, and the Colt exploded vainly in the air as it was torn out of his grasp. The speed of the stallion was tremendous by this time. Life was, for Duff Gregor, a blur of green and blue that darted past his eyes altogether too fast for him to make sure he was alive and a creature capable of thought.

Then a man's voice called out. The terrific speed diminished. It ceased.

Gregor rose staggering to his feet and, with spinning sight, saw before him an image, very blurred, of the golden stallion coming eagerly to the hand of a tall man, who was saying: "Steady, boy. Steady, Parade."

Gregor had the rope off his leg, by this time, and the sound of the horse's name knocked the last of his dizziness out of his wits.

"Parade?" he shouted. "Is that Parade?"

He pointed. The great horse stood at the side of his master, staring at the stranger with blazing eyes. The man was big, with heavy, capable shoulders and a body strung out lean and sinewy as that of an Indian runner below the chest. He had a big head and a big, brown, handsome face.

"This is Parade," he was saying. "Are you hurt?"

"Parade?" echoed Gregor. "Then you're Arizona Jim—you're Jim Silver!"

"I can't say 'No' to that," replied the other.

Gregor was not easily amused, but now he broke into rather wild laughter.

"Wouldn't I do it?" he cried, when he was able to speak again. "Wouldn't I try to rope a Parade? Wouldn't it be my luck to run into that horse in a range all filled with mustangs?" Silver said nothing, and suddenly Gregor was explaining.

"There wasn't a mark of a saddle or a bridle on him. No saddle gall. I thought he was a wild one, Silver." He advanced, holding out his hand. "Name is Duff Gregor," he said. "Sorry I daubed the rope on your stallion, Silver. My mustang is in a junk heap, 'way back yonder."

Silver took his hand freely. Gregor noted that there was no hesitation. Considering the number of men who would have been glad to freeze onto the gun hand of such a man and pump lead into him at the same instant, this might have appeared rather strange, had it not been that Gregor knew perfectly well that Silver was about as good with the left hand as with the right. And there he stood, shaking hands with Jim Silver!

Little worms of ice wriggled up and down his spine. It would be something to tell his cronies, that he had stood face to face with that perennial and terrible enemy of gun fighters and thugs in general. That he had looked into the face and the eyes of this eagle who preyed on hawks only. That he had held the hand of Jim Silver and had seen the scars that streaked his skin.

Yes, the story was true. There were a dozen—no, there were twenty little gleams of brightness in the face of Silver. Bullets had cut the flesh or drilled through it. Knives had done their share. Such danger as he had made his bedfellow could not be endured for many years without leaving its marks.

In fact, there was a whole pattern of war on the face of Jim Silver, very dimly sketched in, to be sure, but visible to a keen eye when the slant light of such a sun as this fell straight against the skin.

Duff Gregor pumped that terrible hand three times, and with each gesture he thought of the number of times the thumb that now pressed the back of his knuckles had fanned the hammer of a revolver and sent death into the hearts of greater men than Duff Gregor would ever claim to be.

He could see that everything he had heard was true, and from the gesture, the voice, of this man, he knew that his modesty was as great as his daredevil courage. He was one of those quiet fellows who fight their battles only once and forget the past before their revolvers are cold. That was Jim Silver. An unwilling admiration and an envious, grim passion rose in the heart of the card cheat, gunman, and general crook.

It was unfair that there should be such a fellow on the face of the earth. Ordinarily, one could say that the so-called "good" men simply lacked the courage to take chances and get illegal gains. But one or two such fellows as Jim Silver were enough to explode the theory. He loved a square deal as he loved danger.

"By thunder, Jim," said Gregor, "there's something about you! Maybe I've seen your picture before, but it looks to me as though I've known you, somewhere!"

"Does it?" asked Jim Silver, with a faint smile.

Duff Gregor had heard of that smile, too, the faintness of it which was rarely brightened or dimmed by circumstances. No man who wore that smile could be called a habitually happy man. Gregor was savagely glad of it. He heard Silver continuing:

"You've looked in your mirror and you know yourself, Gregor. And we're a lot alike."

"You mean that?" exclaimed Gregor.

"Of course. We're about of a build, and our faces are a good deal alike. We could pass for brothers, Gregor, I suppose."

Brothers?

Gregor thought of a past that ranged from sneak thieving to cheating at cards and an occasional plain stick-up; he thought of the long record of the brave and honorable actions of Silver, and a chilly shudder went through him. Yes, it was true that they looked very much alike, if one could read only skin deep.

"Well, I'll be hanged!" said Gregor, gasping.

"I hope not," said Silver, and his smile was fainter than ever.

CHAPTER 2

Stage Holdup

They camped together. Duff Gregor never forgot that occasion. He never forgot his bewilderment when, at Silver's chosen point on the runlet of water, the fire was built and a bit of fresh venison was started roasting after it had been cut into convenient chunks and spitted on bits of wood, for then he discovered that Jim Silver traveled through the land with no further provision than a rifle, salt, and matches!

"Why," said Gregor, "a wild goose couldn't fly no lighter than that! How'd you bed yourself down, brother?"

"I have a blanket and a slicker," said Silver.

It was true. One threadbare blanket and a slicker; that was all.

"When I have to move, I generally have to move fast—and sometimes rather far," explained Silver.

That was true, also. A thousand crooks of all sorts and sizes, most of them dangerous, because Silver never bothered with small fry, were constantly on the lookout for opportunities to revenge themselves on this man.

Many a time, according to legend, they had banded together and, in full power, hunted Jim Silver north and south and east and west. Parade was what beat them, and when they scattered, Parade bore his master on the back trail until some two or three of the pursuers had paid for their rashness as much as man can pay. These

14

man hunts had grown unpopular, therefore, among Silver's greatest enemies.

But it was more than the need to escape enemies or the will to hunt them down that made Silver fly light. Men said that he could not find continued happiness in any one spot, as though there were a curse upon him, and he was forced to rove endlessly. Or perhaps he was seeking happiness as other men seek for gold, and never finding more than the brief content that comes from action.

There were other reasons, later on, why Gregor could never forget the evening, or the picture of the calm, quiet face of Jim Silver. He had sense enough not to turn the conversation on the past, or to try to make Silver talk about his exploits. He knew the man's reputation for taciturnity in all that concerned his own feats. But he found that Silver would talk readily enough in a deep, pleasantly flowing voice. What he liked to describe were his journeys through the mountains or across the deserts, and the strange men he had met—old pioneers, squatters, Indians—who partook of the nature of the wilderness and of the frontier life.

Silver went to bed early. He simply took his blanket and slicker and went off, after he had first cut a good soft bed of evergreen boughs and saplings for Gregor.

"I have to keep in the open," said Silver. "People could sneak up on me, if I stayed in cover like this. But out in the open Parade takes care of me. And I've learned to sleep warm enough with one blanket and a slicker—even in the snow."

He went out, in fact, on the bare flat of the valley, and there gaping Gregor saw him lie down, while the great stallion ranged to and fro.

No doubt Parade himself lay down before morning, but the last Gregor saw of the picture Parade was still moving about, now and then nibbling the grass, and again throwing up his head to study the far horizon and all of the unseen dangers of sound and scent that blew to him down the wind.

Well, it would take a clever man to stalk Jim Silver under conditions like these. But not even for the devotion of a matchless horse like that would Duff Gregor have changed conditions with Silver, and not for all the fame that rang in the ears of men. To eat like a wild hawk, and live like a wild hawk—that was not for Gregor!

How could Jim Silver enter a town without being aware, every instant, that danger might leap at him from every doorway, that guns might fire from every window? How could he sit in peace, except with two walls of a room guarding his back? What, in fact, did life mean to such a man, except the arduous pursuit of glory, unendingly?

Gregor had asked during the evening: "D'you like it, Jim? D'you like living this sort of a life—traveling with no coffee, no flour, no bacon, no cooking pans, no nothing?"

And Silver had said: "Well, it makes everything more simple. I used to carry not even salt, but I've added that. I guess I'm getting old and soft. But you can look at it this way, Duff: Wherever you go, no matter on what desert, there's always life of some sort. There aren't very many desert jack rabbits, but there are some. Wherever you go, you'll find game, if you hunt carefully for it. And if you miss food for a couple of days, it makes it taste all the better when you make a kill."

It was a very simple philosophy, but it made the heart of Duff Gregor grow small. For himself, he preferred a little more fat, a little more comfort, a little less glory, if need be. But to think of lying down every night without the certainty that the day would ever dawn again—that the bark of a gun or the cold agony of steel buried in the throat might not be the end of the world!

No wonder that this man had been able to run even the great criminal name of Barry Christian out of the world, and broken him utterly, and his gang, too, so that one heard nothing of Christian in these days.

It might be that Christian was dead. It might be that, a broken man, he was cooking for some obscure cattle ranch. But no wonder that Silver had beaten him, for the man was all edge. He was all cutting edge: he could not fail to win.

When Gregor rose in the morning, the fire had already been rekindled by Silver, and they had for breakfast the same as they had had the night before. At least, Gregor had it.

"Roast meat and cold water," he said. "How d'you stand it? Ain't it monotonous?"

"You see," said Silver, "when I'm on the range, I eat only once a day, and then I'm so hungry that I'm never tired of meat. And I'm so thirsty that water tastes better than wine."

That day he took Gregor across the mountains through the first pass. In the middle of the day he showed him a patch of houses on the other side of a valley.

"That's Allerton," said Silver. "The stage from Crow's Nest runs there. If you want to move on, you can get the stage. Any money?"

There was plenty of money in the pocket of Gregor, but he had no objection to taking more. He said that unluckily he was broke.

Silver took a sheaf of five twenties out of his pocket and handed them over. There was very little left of his roll after he had made this contribution. He was easy. It was no wonder that he could not keep the fortunes which he had made several times, because everyone knew that he could not say "No." He was so easy that it was hard for Gregor to keep from laughing in his face.

There was a good wind blowing up the valley, and Silver had taken off his hat to enjoy the coolness of it, and Gregor saw above the temples the two spots of gray hair like horns beginning to push through the hair. Men said that that was how he had first got his name of "Silver-tip" or "Silver."

They shook hands, and then Gregor marched down the slope and up the other side. Before he had gone far on his way, Silver had disappeared. The great waste of the mountains had received him again. Where would he reappear? Only where the needs of some unlucky man or the outrage committed by some criminal called him out of his quiet seclusion.

Gregor climbed on into Allerton, went into the first saloon, and leaned a heavy elbow on the bar until he had poured three drinks under his belt. After that, he was able to stop thinking.

"To blazes with Jim Silver!" he said under his breath, and went to a restaurant to find food. Finally, when he had well filled himself, the thought of that lonely soul who drifted through mountains hunting for happiness with a deathless and futile hope grew dim in his brain.

He looked over Allerton, decided that it offered few opportunities for a man of his genius, and, therefore, took the two-o'clock stage for Crow's Nest, which was far off in the blue of the next range toward the west. Crow's Nest was a big town, a booming town, men told him. There were mines not far from it. Lumbering went on near by. Moreover, a certain number of tenderfeet were attracted by the mineral waters of a hot spring that bubbled up in the center of the town, and a good many sick people were constantly in Crow's Nest, taking a cure.

It was exactly the sort of a spot that Gregor liked to haunt, for wherever you find invalids, you find reckless spending. No one, he knew, spends so much money having a good time as the man who expects that he may be dead before morning. The death house atmosphere of such a town would be exactly suited to the peculiar talents of Gregor.

So he took the two-o'clock stage and found himself with six other passengers. Every one of them seemed to be a step up from the average population of Allerton. Their baggage looked like "money inside."

When he was sure of this, he felt more at ease than ever. It was a new part of the range, for him. He had never been within five hundred miles of it before he had come to Piute, and Duff Gregor liked new things. He liked new faces, new whisky, new money, and new guns. He liked everything new except new jails.

He felt that this world is a comfortable place. The sun was a shade more brilliant, more warm, more pleasing to the soul, with its golden radiance, than ever before. It shone alike upon the just and the unjust, but he felt that the unjust had just an edge of advantage. How many crooks in this world, for instance, could say that they had twice eaten food cooked by the immortal, man-slaying hands of Jim Silver, lived with him for a day, and parted from him a hundred dollars up?

It was only fifty miles to Crow's Nest. The first part of the journey spun out behind the heels of the galloping horses at the rate of fifteen miles an hour, but the long up-tug toward the town in the next range had to be taken at a walk, and the afternoon had worn away toward sunset, with the sun drifting beside them like fire in the branches of the pine trees, and the sweeter scent and the cooler breath of evening was already coming into the air when, as they turned a corner, a rifle shot clanged like two heavy sledge hammers struck face to face.

The near leader of the team dropped dead. From behind a rock rose the head and shoulders of a masked man who was peering down a very steady rifle.

"Stick 'em up, boys," he said. "Keep 'em right over your heads. Try to touch the sky all the time, and step out on this side, please. Driver, watch yourself, or—"

The rifle spat thin smoke. Its muzzle jerked. The driver cursed and grabbed his right shoulder.

"Sorry," said the highwayman. "You shouldn't have made that move, brother."

There was no mistaking his professional manner. Gregor and all the rest gave up hope of resistance on the spot. Nothing discourages action so much as the sight of blood. Gregor was muttering quietly, "My rotten luck!" as he climbed out to the ground and stood in line with the others.

CHAPTER 3

Barry Christian

The stage driver seemed to be a fool. He insisted on going forward to look at his near leader. The masked man warned him grimly:

"Brother, if you budge one more step, I'll shoot a few inches inside that first slug."

The driver turned and scowled at him. He was a big fellow, that driver. He had rusty red hair and a big, saber-shaped mustache.

"I ain't got a gun," he said. "I was reachin' for a chaw of tobacco a while back, not for a gun. Go and fan me for a Colt, if you wanta, but I gotta see if you been and murdered Molly." With that, he walked right past the leveled gun of the robber and went to the dead horse. The rifle of the masked man hesitated just as his mind must have hesitated. Then he said:

"Perhaps you're right, old-timer. Now, boys, kindly turn your backs, while I make a change."

The "change" consisted of tossing the rifle aside and at the same instant pulling out a revolver. This weapon he held only hip-high and did not aim with his eye on the sights. There *were* no sights, in fact, and instead of curving a forefinger around the trigger, the right thumb of the robber rested on the hammer of his gun. It was perfectly plain that here was a fellow who knew how to fan a revolver, and such men are not the ones to take liberties with.

Everybody in that party seemed sufficiently experienced to know all about the trick and the quality of the man who can perform it. Not one of the passengers attempted violence with the robber. All turned their backs obediently, and the highwayman went down the line, clapping the muzzle of the gun against the spinal columns, while with a marvelously rapid left hand he "frisked" every pocket. No pocket, in fact, was too secret for him to find it. He threw on the ground everything he secured—guns, wallets, knives—except the big, fat gold watches, which he dropped into his own pockets. He found stickpins and gold cuff links. Everything was secured with wonderful skill and rapidity by this master hand.

Then he told the youngest of the party to climb up behind the stage and cut the straps that held the baggage. Down into the road tumbled the luggage. A cloud of dust rose, and with it groans from two or three of the unlucky passengers.

"Sorry, boys," said the robber. "I have to go through this stuff to see what's what, but nothing is going to be spoiled on purpose. I want valuables, not clothes, and if you'll send back here for the stuff after an hour, you'll collect what's left. If anyone tries to come back *before* an hour, I'll show him that when I touched the driver on the shoulder, I was doing it on purpose—not missing my mark. I'm a man of a quiet temper, fellows, but I'm apt to lose hold of myself if any of you rush back to this place. Driver, cut loose that off leader. He only imbalances your team now, and besides I need him."

The driver, without a word, unhooked the off leader, pulled the harness off it with his left hand—the right hung helpless from his wounded shoulder—and unhooked the doubletrees from the fifth chain. Then he paused and looked down at the dead gray mare.

"There's a mare," said the driver, "that never said 'No.' There's a mare that knew every curve of the road from here to Crow's Nest. I been drunk behind her, and she's made better time when

I was drunk than when I was sober. If a gent had the sense to use the brake, she had the sense to take the curves. There's a mare, boys, that was a lady, and I loved her."

He came back toward the stage. One of the men offered to tie up his wound.

He answered: "Climb up there and haul on the brake for me, when I speak up. I'll take care of the line. I don't need no doctor till I get to Crow's Nest. I dunno that I wanta be touched by any one of the seven skunks that'll let one crook stick 'em up. There's too much yaller poison in your systems. I wouldn't wanta risk some of it runnin' into mine."

Tears were on his face as he spoke. He let them roll, unheeded. He climbed back into the seat, and the rest of the men prepared to follow. The youngster of the lot got up to handle the brake. Then the voice of the robber said:

"You, there—back up! You stay with me!"

All turned. The muzzle of the revolver definitely picked out Duff Gregor from the lot.

"You want *me?*" exclaimed Gregor, with a chill in his soul.

"You!" said the robber. "And keep your hands up! If you try to move, I'll plaster you. You fool, I know you!" What did that mean?

With dull eyes, Gregor watched the stage start off. With ringing ears, he heard the departing curses which the passengers hurled behind them at the robber.

The masked man knew him? Well, there was a great deal in this life of Gregor. There was enough to fill ten columns of fine print, and nothing but facts mentioned. Some victim of a card game, someone who had been "rolled" by Gregor when the victim was drunk?

The stage rumbled out of view behind the next bend of the road. Then the highwayman came up and shoved the muzzle of his revolver into Duff's middle. He said, in a voice which emotion made ring like a bell: "I've had you in my hands twice. This is the third time, and it's the last. Don't you know me?"

"I don't know you," said Gregor.

There was silence.

"You're changed," said the highwayman. "You're almost so changed that I wouldn't know you. But I really believe that you don't recognize me. If *I* were you, I'd know by the voice alone, but if you want to see my face, take a look at it, Jim Silver!"

With that he ripped the mask away.

Gregor's starting eyes stared into a finely made face, a long, handsome face. It had a sensitive, a mobile and almost delicate look, except that there was something infinitely cruel about the mouth and the bright, steady eyes. And the long, silken hair flowed back after the style that so many artists affect.

"It doesn't look so good to you, Jim, eh?" said the stranger. "It doesn't seem possible that the great Jim Silver would shove up his hands in a stage-coach and let any one man rob him, eh? But here you stand, ten seconds from death, Jim! I can't believe that it's the end of the long trail, at last. And if I hang for this tomorrow, I'll die a happy man!"

And Gregor knew, with wonderful certainty, that he was, in fact, hardly a scant ten seconds away from the future world. He had to think fast, and his mind was luckily one that fear stimulated and did not benumb.

"Brother," he said, "you got me wrong. I've got a shadow over my face just now, but lemme turn west into the light, and then see if I wear the scars of Jim Silver."

"Ah?" said the other, and started violently. He took Gregor by the left shoulder and turned him hastily toward the west, where the light fell more closely on his face. Then he snarled with disgust and rage.

"I should have known!" he said. "I should have guessed it wasn't Jim Silver standing for a one-man play like mine. But who gave you a face so much like his?"

"Brother," said Gregor, "my face may be like his, but I've never made one phony dime out of the resemblance."

"It's not so like, either, now that I take another look," said the robber. "I suppose that hope was making me blind. But," he added, "you're close enough to turn your face into a mint! At least, it would be good for a million in this part of the world!"

"Because I look like Silver?" said Gregor. "Hold on, old-timer. A little confidence work, you mean? Maybe, in the end, I'm going to be glad that you stopped that stage. All at once some ideas seem to begin to soak into my brain."

There was silence between them, each man reading the mind of the other.

"What's your lay?" asked the robber shortly.

"Anything," said Duff Gregor, with a frankness which he felt would do him no harm, under the circumstances. "Anything from a jimmy to a gun is good enough for me, and I know how to make a mold with yellow soap and mine the soup in it, if you come to cases."

There followed another silence, then the stranger asked: "Have you got an idea who I am?"

"Not the foggiest idea," said Gregor. "You might be Barry Christian, for all I know."

"Might be?" said the other. "Everyone knows my face has been published up and down the land. Everyone knows the publishing of it—and Silver's dirty work—has started me on the road like a common tramp of a stick-up artist. But if you have half an eye in your head, you'll see that I *am* Christian."

CHAPTER 4

A Foundation Stone

Afterward, they sat by a fire twenty miles away, on the farther side of Crow's Nest. Christian had had his own mount of course, and the stage line horse had carried Gregor from the scene of the hold-up. Those twenty miles, Barry Christian had insisted upon, and Gregor knew better than to dispute the will or the way of that famous man. For Barry Christian was a master of the art of breaking the law with impunity, as he had proved many times during the long course of his celebrated career. No penalties had fallen to his share, except those which had become his through that still greater man, Jim Silver.

It had not taken long for Christian and Gregor to come to an agreement. One of the most amazing parts of the affair was the speed with which Christian looked through the mind of his new acquaintance. It was as though he knew all about the furnishings of the mind of Gregor and exactly how far Gregor would go. He repeatedly turned his back on Gregor, as he was working about the campfire or attending to the horses.

That was a risky business, because, no matter how awed Gregor might be by the reputation of his new friend, it was also true that there were fifteen thousand dollars on the head of Barry Christian. And for the cost of one little leaden bullet, all of that fortune would be transferred to the hands of Gregor!

It would not take much—a flick of the hand and a jerk of the thumb or forefinger, and Barry Christian and all his famous past and all of his great deeds would lie dead on the ground. It would not only make Gregor rich for the time being, but it would swell his reputation into a formidable size. His own past would be forgiven. He would be mentioned in every newspaper. Reporters would travel three thousand miles for the sake of shaking his hand and snapping his picture, and picking up a few of his wise sayings. Men would write the story of his life, adroitly covering over the evil, and changing sheer crime into clear adventure, for this is undoubtedly true—that the world loves an adventurer and has an almost unsurpassable wish to believe well of him.

These conclusions kept working in the mind of Gregor, but still his hand was held. The same thought had been in his mind when he was with Jim Silver, to tell the truth. To be known as the slayer of Silver would give him a vast name among crooks all over the world. But a certain freezing awe had numbed the powers of his hand, when he thought of Christian, and it annoyed him to see that Christian seemed to understand his superiority and that the outlaw was able to count on it.

After a time, the irritation passed out of the mind of Gregor. He was soothed and pleased by what he could call his great good luck. Fate, he considered, does not mean badly by the man whom he brings to the side of Jim Silver one night, and Barry Christian the next. It even occurred to Gregor that it was like one of the old legends in which the hero is brought to the crossing of the ways and told to select either the straight and narrow path or the rosy way to evil. Gregor had two sorts of life to choose from—that of Jim Silver or that of Barry Christian.

There was no doubt in his mind as to which course he would take. The mere thought of Silver's way of existence made an arctic ache of cold grip his soul, but with Barry Christian he lolled in comfort. He understood the man more nearly.

For one thing, Christian was not the fellow to live like an ascetic. He brought out a good cooking set of pots and pans, and he prepared as delightful a supper as one could ask for in a camp. There was even pan bread, instead of tooth-cracking hardtack.

What pleased Gregor more than the good food was the pleasant manner of Barry Christian. The man's handsome, mobile face was continually smiling, and his soft voice was a music in the ears of Gregor. Also, Christian talked with disarming frankness.

As they smoked cigarettes and sipped the good strong coffee which Christian had made, while the firelight tossed far-traveling gleams through the corridors of the pines and a troubled squirrel came out to argue angrily from a branch above, Christian said:

"You see that I've dropped a long distance downhill, Gregor. I'm reduced to common stick-up work, these days. I used to do better things. I used to be able to sit back and plan real jobs in a real manner. But that's changed. D'you know why?"

"No," said Gregor.

"Jim Silver broke me," said Christian, looking Gregor straight in the eye. "He beat me twice, and the second time that he smashed me, all my old men lost confidence in me. It began to look to them as though I were no good for rainy weather. They got out from under. However, I managed to make out."

He had been sorting the loot that he had collected from the stage, as he talked. It had been a pretty good haul, on the whole. After the suit-cases had been searched—and then, according to promise, neatly reclosed and stacked beside the road—there was a total of over five thousand dollars in hard cash, to say nothing of a good heap of watches and stickpins and other jewelry. Christian put a thousand dollars and a portion of the "hardware" into the hands of Gregor.

"What for?" asked Gregor, gasping.

"You were on hand for the finish," said Christian. "I always make a split with anyone who's on my side."

"On your side? I would have plastered you with a ton of lead, if I'd seen my chance," said Gregor frankly.

"That was before we really knew one another," answered Christian. "Don't argue, Gregor. You're in the game with me, and you're welcome to a split. It isn't hard cash that I look for so much as other things, in this work. I don't want a lone hand. I want to build from the bottom until I'm bigger than I ever was before, and you'll be my first foundation stone, if you want to come in."

Duff Gregor stared down at his split of the plunder and drew in a breath. Then, without a word, he put away his loot in his clothes.

"But," explained the outlaw, "I only want you if you feel that you're my man."

"Why, Christian," said Gregor, "how can I help being your man? We're together if you say the word. I'm not such a fool as to turn you down. I know your record, man—part of it, anyway." Then he added: "But what makes you want me in? You don't know me."

"I can read a man pretty well when I have a chance to look at him down the sights of a gun," answered Christian.

He ran his long fingers through the flowing silk of his hair. As the cold of the evening began, he had wrapped a scarf around his throat, and he seemed, now, a very romantic figure, indeed. Gregor thought that he had never seen a more handsome or capable face.

Christian went on: "There's another reason. No man could look so much like Jim Silver without having a brain in his head."

"Has Silver a lot of brains?" asked Gregor.

Christian looked sharply at him, as though suspecting that he was being drawn on. "Silver's beaten me twice," he said simply. "That's enough brains for any man's nut to hold."

"But what does he make out of beating you?" asked Gregor. "He travels around like a lone wolf that's been thrown out of the pack. He eats like a beggar and dresses like a tramp; and he's in as much danger, when he goes to a town, as anybody who's outside the law. What does he get out of life?"

"Well," said Barry Christian, "no matter what the danger, he goes where he pleases. He follows his own wish around the world. He rides the finest horse in the West, and tucked away, here and there, are rich men and poor men he can bank on if he needs them—fellows who would die for him if he gave them a chance and a call."

"But he never gives 'em a chance," said Gregor. "He plays his hand all alone. I'd call it a fool's life."

"Because you and I," said Christian, "don't like what's meat to him."

"He hasn't even a woman he's fond of," said Gregor, "according to what people say."

"The girl he's in love with," answered Christian, "is a lady with very bright eyes, old son—eyes so bright that they dazzle most of us more than diamonds. Danger is her name, and she's what Silver lives for."

Gregor was silent, brooding on the matter.

"Silver's done so much," said Christian, "that his name is known all over the West. And in the East, too, I suppose. Not many people have seen him, because of the way he lives, but he's a man whose name is strong enough to move mountains."

"How?" asked Gregor.

Christian was silent, smoking, thinking. Then he asked: "Gregor, are you with me?"

"Till the last card falls," said Gregor. "We'll shake on that."

Their hands closed together. The eyes of Gregor blinked under the stare of Christian, and he knew, as he confronted the man, that that handshake was a turning point in his life. He had lived very much as he pleased before this. Now he felt that he had hitched himself to a comet that might snatch him to death in an instant. But there was the sort of manhood in Gregor that responded to the challenge and thrilled with it.

"Now listen to me," said Christian. "You have the general build of Silver. You're not quite so much in the shoulders and not quite so lean in the hips. You don't look so much like a panther in good training. But there's a big resemblance. Your face isn't the same, aside from the scars, but the features are very much alike. Enough for me to make a mistake in the half light at the end of today, and that's one face in the world that should be familiar to me. If you can pass me in a half light, you can pass nearly everybody else in the full light of day. And out of that resemblance, you ought to be able to move mountains."

"How?" asked Gregor.

"We'll need to touch you up a bit," said Christian. "For one thing, a couple of gray spots have to appear in your hair above the temples. For another thing, we'll need to make a few scars appear on your face. I can manage both things in a couple of hours so that it would take a microscope to tell that it's a fake. You need one other thing—you need a horse like Parade."

"Then I'm beaten," said Gregor. "I've seen that big chunk of lightning, and I know there's no other like him."

"You're wrong," answered Christian. "I can put my hand on a thoroughbred chestnut stallion with the whole look of Parade about him. Not half an inch smaller, not fifty pounds lighter, and carries himself like a champion. He's on a ranch, not far from here—not twenty miles from here, in fact."

"Four black stockings all around?" demanded Gregor.

"Only one. But what are dyes for, Gregor? I tell you, I can get that horse for two or three thousand dollars, and with you on his back—after you and the horse have been touched up—you can ride into any town in the West and open it up like a nutshell.

Along with you will be Barry Christian, looking like a tired old man, and between us we'll take the golden lining out of any place we name. What's the matter with Crow's Nest, with one of the biggest banks in a thousand miles of us?"

The light had dawned in the eyes of Gregor. Now he threw up his hands with a whoop. "By jove, you're right, and the world's our oyster!" he shouted.

CHAPTER 5

At Crow's Nest

Not many days after that, a thrill went through Crow's Nest, from its smallest outlying shack to the new, big stone buildings of its main street, and then up the slopes on either side to the huge hotel on the one hand and to the hotel-casino-bathing establishment on the other, where the invalids from the North, South, and East came to be "cured." There was not very much to be said in favor of that spring water, but it had a taste of sulphur and a few other minerals in it, and a few quack doctors and a great deal of faith now and again worked marvelous cures. Where the faith is strong, the flesh can never be very weak.

The excitement that ran like a flame through Crow's Nest and brought tradesmen away from their counters, and every boy and girl into the street, and men and women crowding into doors and windows, was all centered around two horsemen who came slowly up the main street.

One of them was a fellow with long white hair and a face set off by beetling black brows and a short-cropped black mustache. A scar pulled one cheek and twisted his mouth a little toward a sneering smile, and yet it was a handsome face, after all, and the texture of the skin was surprisingly young for one wearing white hair. He was dressed in a battered old gray suit, and he rode a dusty mule, his body slumping forward in the saddle and his chin thrusting outward a little. When the mule trotted, his elbows flapped up and down, as a proof that he was not at all at home in the saddle.

He was not the attraction, however. In fact, he won hardly a glance. What counted was the magnificent figure of the man on the prancing chestnut stallion, which sweated and danced all over the street and thereby enabled the rider to show off to better advantage the graces of his horsemanship.

He was a big young man with a brown, handsome face that was streaked here and there with the silver of old scars. All around him poured the boys of the town. They swirled about him, shouting and leaping. Their more tardy companions, who had the news at a greater distance, were bringing dust clouds down the street as they rushed to join the procession. Some of the smaller boys reached for the stirrups of the rider. They seemed fearless even of the dancings of the horse.

The older people in the community were hardly less enthusiastic. The men of the West seldom shed their dignity, but dignity was forgotten now. Here and there an enthusiast fired a gun into the air and gave a cowboy yell.

An old man came hobbling on crutches to the gate of his front yard and waved his hat and shouted: "Jim Silver! Three cheers for Arizona Jim!"

At this, the rider took off his hat and made a bow over his saddle, and there was more cheering, and a woman's shrill voice yipped: "It's Silver! I seen the gray spots, just like little horns! But there's no devil in Jim Silver!" The whole street was washed by a wave of greater tumult, every moment, but all of the excitement was not exactly happy.

Out of the hotel doorway ran a tall man with a sweeping black mustache. He carried a half-rolled blanket which he threw over the withers of a horse, and, mounting, with the tails of his long coat flapping behind him, he galloped hastily up the street, away from the disturbance. His big-brimmed gray Stetson blew off, but he did not pause to pick it up. He made tracks as fast as his horse could carry him.

There were others who took horses here and there and seemed to be answering an inaudible summons that took them toward the tall timber. Gamblers, confidence men, thugs of various sorts had heard the cheering for Jim Silver, and to every one of them it seemed that a gun had been pointed at his head. For no man could tell on what errands Silver rode, except to be sure that the end of his trail would be the punishment of crime of one sort or another. It was best to take no chances with him. Chances taken with Jim Silver were too apt to end in fatalities.

The impersonation given by the rider of the brilliant chestnut stallion was not perfect, however. As he went on, the white-haired man found a chance to swing his mule close to the chestnut and say, under his breath: "Don't stick out your chest like a fool! Remember Jim Silver's the most modest man in the world, Gregor!"

"All right, Barry," said Gregor, and promptly brought the pace of his horse down a bit, and sat a shade less like a conqueror in the saddle.

The pair of them drew up in front of the hotel, where the horse and mule were tethered. A man hurried up to them, saying: "Say, Jim Silver, you know that the big hotels are up on the hill. You go up there. This here ain't the best that Crow's Nest can offer you."

"Thanks, partner," Gregor answered, "but you take a big hotel and it always means a big bill. I ain't so flush with coin, d'you see? I guess this place is going to suit me pretty well."

The proprietor of the hotel had managed to get out to the sidewalk all in a sweat, by this time. He was a fat little man, now flushed with excitement, and he grabbed the arm of Gregor and escorted him proudly into the lobby.

He called out, as he came in: "Hey, Mr. Watson, if you don't mind moving, I'm going to give your corner room to Jim Silver and move you to the back. Mind?"

"No, sir," said Watson, standing up, tall and gangling, from his chair. He grew bright red with pleasure. "It ain't much that a gent ever has a chance to do for Jim Silver, and if I had ten rooms, I reckon that he could have them all."

Gregor had turned with a grin toward Watson, when Christian kicked him sharply on the ankle, muttering:

"Refuse, you fool!"

"Thanks, Mr. Watson," said Gregor; "I can't take your room. About the best place for me is going to be a back room somewhere. I don't much care where. Quiet—and not too many windows—is what I'd rather have."

"And *that's* a pity," said the proprietor. "Watson's room has three windows and—"

"You know, partner," said Gregor, breaking in, "that three guns can look in through three windows, and a gent can only look out of one window at a time."

There was a big laugh at this. Gregor joined heartily in the mirth until Christian stepped on his toes. Then he bit his lip and subsided.

They registered as James Silver and Thomas Bennett, then they were taken upstairs to pick out their room. A little back room with two cots in it was selected by Gregor after he had received a warning look from Christian. A moment later they were alone together, after the proprietor had assured them that there would be no charge to Jim Silver and company so long as they cared to stay, an offer which Gregor was again forced to refuse by a nudge from Christian.

Now that they were alone, Christian locked the door and slumped into a chair. With a cold, bright eye he stared at his companion.

"What's the matter, Barry?" asked Gregor. "You look as though I'd missed in the spelling bee."

"No," said Christian slowly. "No, you haven't failed. It's all right. Almost anything would be all right so long as you're the fellow who's doing it. You could marry any girl in the town if you cared to smile at her twice. You could have any man's horse, dog, gun, or money for the asking. You could stay on forever in the best hotel and never have a bill sent in to you. You could sit in a corner the rest of your days and still be looked on as a public benefactor. And why? Because you're made up to look like Jim Silver, and because Jim Silver has used his guns on the side of the law."

He left his chair and paced rapidly, softly, back and forth through the room. Plainly, he was smoking with subdued passion.

"They'd die for him in a crowd," said Barry Christian. "They love the ground he walks on. But maybe they'll feel a little more sketchy about the wonders of Jim Silver before you and I are through with them. Maybe they'll understand that a name can cover more than one face. Man, how I hate them all! Every time they yelled for Silver it was just like a knife stuck into me."

He leaned on the window sill and stared at the sweep of the great pine trees that climbed up the mountainside toward the glittering white of the health resort at the top of the slope.

"I know," said Gregor, nodding. "It makes a gent sick to see people go nutty about some bum. Barry, I'm the king of this here town for a while. How'd I take the job?"

Christian turned back on him. He controlled himself for an instant before he spoke. "I've told you that you did well enough," he said, "but you forget a great many of the things that I told you. Silver speaks grammatical English. You're apt to talk like a cross between an ignorant cowhand and a schoolteacher. Silver has the manner of a fellow who's almost afraid of a crowd; you act like an actor waiting for a curtain call. You keep your head in the air and look around with a silly grin. Silver looks at the floor and hardly smiles at all. When he looks a man in the eye, the man is apt to remember the hour and the day the rest of his life. Silver acts like a modest man.

"You have to remember, all the time, that you're not yourself. You have to try to force yourself into a new frame of mind. You have to try to enlarge your heart and soul, and make yourself think that you're both brave and gentle. Silver is a man who wouldn't take a penny from the Bank of England; he'd fight a lion with his bare hands; and he'd die for any cause that seemed the right thing to him. Brother, you and I are not men of that type, but you'll have to try to expand to an extra size. Understand?"

"I understand," said the other gloomily. There was a knock at the door.

Christian waved the fake Jim Silver aside and unlocked the door. The proprietor was standing there holding a note, wanting to know if everything was all right.

"There's a gent downstairs that wrote this out. Wants to see Jim Silver," he said.

"Silver's all knocked out," said Christian loudly, after he had read the note. "Jim is lying down, resting. It's the first sleep he's had in a long while, and he needs it. Tell Taxi that he wants to see him, that he's wild to see him—tell him that from me, but say that I won't let anybody near Jim Silver till he's had at least a couple of hours' rest."

"I'll tell him. I'll satisfy him. Is he a friend of Jim Silver?"

"He is. He's an old friend, I guess," said Christian.

"Then he can have the whole house if he wants it," said the proprietor, and departed. Christian turned from the newly locked door with a groan.

"Trouble right at the start," said Christian. "Everything's ruined, I guess."

"Why? Who's this Taxi, anyway? Is he someone who knows Silver?"

"Knows him? Taxi knows him like a brother. Taxi is the crook who came out of the East with the soul of a wild Indian, the manners and the kindness of a wildcat, and a crooked reputation as long as your arm. Silver reformed him. Silver took him out of my hands, and then when I had Silver tied and as good as dead, Taxi cut him loose from me. I won't go into that yarn. I'll simply tell you that we've got our backs against the wall, flat! Taxi is only a split second slower than Silver on the draw and a shade quieter in the brain, but he's fast enough both ways to keep us both on the run. Gregor, you have a brain and a good pair of hands. So have I. Let's get ready to use everything we own!"

CHAPTER 6

Taxi Calls

Christian got to the window in a stride and pulled down the shade. He picked up the hat he had thrown down and drew it well over his eyes, saying, in the meantime: "Kick off your boots, throw off your coat, pull off your trousers, pile into that bed."

Gregor obeyed with speed, merely asking: "What's the main line of Taxi?"

"He can fade through any lock that was ever made," answered Barry Christian. "He can read the mind of nearly any safe, but if he can't read its mind, he can crack it just as easily as he can crack his fingers."

He caught up a pillow and wedged it in close beside the head of Gregor to cast a darker shadow over his face.

"Tell Taxi," said Christian, "that you're in a big job. You want him, but not right away. Tell him to get out of town and wait till you send for him."

"Will he do that?"

"He'll do anything except jump off a cliff for you, so long as he thinks you're Jim Silver." Christian added: "Don't look him in the eyes. He can see in the dark, like a cat. Keep looking down. Play you're dead tired. He can tell you by a touch. He's got eyes in his fingers. No, we can't risk him even shaking hands with you. Here—here are your gloves. Pull them on and—"

Before he could get any further in his warnings and his preparations, there was a tap at the door. It was a light, quick rap of two soft beats, a pause, and a harder blow.

The eye of Barry Christian flashed as he recognized a Signal that must have some meaning to the great Jim Silver.

He went to the door and opened it. Before him stood a slender man of hardly a shade more than middle height, and dressed in a dapper blue suit, with a soft gray hat, and a pair of chamois gloves in his hand. His black hair was sleeked until it glistened. If he had been leaning on a walking stick, he would have served as a fashion advertisement out of a magazine. But Barry Christian had no illusions about the character under that dude exterior.

He held out his hand and pressed the lean, nervous fingers of "Taxi."

"Hello, Taxi," he said in a voice raised only a little above a whisper. "The old man has told me all about you. Silver's knocked out. Listen—don't stay long with him. He's all shot to pieces. Tired, I mean. Come on in."

He backed away, and as he backed up, the slender fellow came with a soundless step through the doorway, and lifting his eyes, which were kept constantly lowered, he gave Christian one pale, bright gleam of inspection. Then he walked on toward the bed, smiling, and holding out his hand.

"Jim, old boy!" he said.

Gregor held out a hand that had a big riding glove on it.

"Covered with rash," he explained, coughing as he spoke. "How are you, Taxi?"

"I'm always on top of the world when I hear that you're anywhere near," said Taxi, sitting down on the edge of the bed. "What's knocked you out?"

Gregor pressed his head all the deeper among the pillows and let his arm fall at his side.

"Been through a lot," he said, in a muffled, groaning voice, "and more trouble ahead." Taxi stood up.

"I'm on deck," he offered.

"Later," said Gregor, carefully maintaining that same groaning voice. "How many people saw you come?"

"About three-outside the hotel. You know I don't walk the main streets when I can possibly help it, Jim."

"Good," muttered Gregor. "If the rats know that you're with me, they may run for cover before I get my teeth in them."

"What rats?" asked Taxi.

"Tell you later. Taxi, will you help?"

"Don't ask. You know."

"Good! Get out of town. Five or ten miles out, and stay put. Wait for me. I'll send you word when I want you. Tell me where you'll be."

Taxi hesitated. Then he said: "There's a broken road that runs straight west of Crow's Nest. Never used. Out there, four or five miles, between a pair of steep hills that bear to the south, there's a little shack. I'll go there and wait, and nobody shall see me leave Crow's Nest, only the people in the hotel here. Can they be trusted?"

"Nobody," said Gregor, shaking his head slowly. "Trust nobody."

Taxi held out his hand. Gregor took it and let his arm fall wearily away again. "So long," said Gregor.

"I wish I could stay here through the pinch," said Taxi, "but you always know best. I'll be out there waiting. I'll have fast horses with me and I'll be ready to jump." He turned to Christian.

"I don't know you, but I've seen you somewhere," said Taxi.

"I'm Thomas Bennett," said Christian, nodding. "I've been around, all right. Maybe you have seen me."

Taxi went to the door, turned there as though he were about to speak once more, and then bent his pale, bright glance on

Christian for another moment. After that, he left the room, and the door made no sound as he shut it behind him.

"Well—" began Duff Gregor.

A frantic signal came from Barry Christian, cutting him short. Another signal made him relax once more in bed. Christian stood transfixed. Even in that dim light, Gregor could see that the face of his famous companion was shining with sweat.

"That's one step behind us, and maybe the longest step of the lot," said Christian in a whisper.

He went to the door and listened for a moment. Then he opened the door and looked into the hall. Turning back, he mopped his face and slumped down into a chair.

"The wildcat!" said Christian. "Did you ever see such a pair of eyes? You can get up now."

"Bored right into me through the shadows," said Gregor.

He sat up and began to pull on his clothes. He, also, had need to wipe his forehead.

"You did it well," said Christian, after a moment of thought. "You couldn't have done it much better. But he suspected something."

"He sure gave you a look, brother," agreed the other.

"There was a ghost walking through his brain just then," answered Christian. "He couldn't put his finger on the right spot in his memory and he probably never will. He can't think of Barry Christian and Jim Silver being together in the same room. The two ideas won't fit. He's in some sort of doubt, but not enough to keep him from doing what you told him to do. That's the way that Silver would act—short sentences and let the other fellow do the guessing. You did it well, Duff, and you didn't slip on your English, either."

"Aw, I can talk as good as anybody, when I get my mind fixed on it," said Duff Gregor.

"Don't you worry about me, brother, when it comes to being slick. Slick enough to skate over the thinnest ice you ever seen."

Christian considered him gravely for a moment and said nothing. He went back to the door, opened it, peered up and down the hall, and returned.

"Walks like a cat too," he said. "He *is* a cat."

"That's how he hit me," said Gregor.

"All the luck in the world," groaned Christian, "couldn't have hitched a more dangerous man to Jim Silver."

"Why can't you buy him off? Give him a big split if he throws in with us?" asked Gregor. Christian stared at him, but then he nodded.

"I understand what you mean," he said. "I used to think the same thing, in the old days. I used to think that every man has his price, but that was before I met Jim Silver. Money's dirt to him. Money's dirt to this handsome young rat of a Taxi. I couldn't buy him if I offered him a diamond as big as my fist."

"It looks to me," said Gregor, "as though we'd better drift out of this town pretty pronto."

The big man nodded. "We have to work fast," he said. "There's that suspicion in the back of Taxi's brain, and he may come back to investigate."

"Suppose," said Gregor, "that he hears how I came prancing into town with the crowd cheering. That won't mate up very well with the way he found me stretched out here."

"That doesn't matter," said Christian. "Taxi knows that Silver could bluff out the devil himself, when it comes to a showdown. Gregor, we have to work fast. But if things go well, before Jim Silver learns of his double here in Crow's Nest, we'll have a fortune in our pockets. And leaving town, we'll drop in at a little shack between a pair of hills four or five miles out of Crow's Nest, and there I'll settle an old score. There'll be one less man in the world when I get through with this job—and Taxi!"

CHAPTER 7

Wilbur's Bank

The rest of that day was spent, presently, in making a little tour of the town, Gregor and Christian riding side by side. Gregor did very well. Perhaps fifty times they were stopped and asked to have a drink at the next saloon, but Gregor always said: "Thanks, but this is my dry time of day."

The only advice that Christian gave him was: "Keep the voice down. Stop gririning, and hardly let yourself smile. Look kind—and tired. That's the nearest you can come to Jim Silver, I'm afraid."

They ate quickly, in a corner of the hotel dining room. It was an empty room when they sat down to eat. It was a crowded room before they had been there for five minutes. Duff Gregor, bathed in this light of another's glory, could hardly keep from thrusting out his chest and exulting. But his companion's quick, stern eye kept him in hand.

A ten-year-old boy with the fore part of his face scrubbed till it was red and shining, while the dust of the day's playing still remained like a fine gray fur over the ears, came up and said: "Mr. Silver, the kids been and challenged me that I wouldn't dare to come in here and shake hands with you, so I come, anyway. My name's Joe Crosby."

Duff Gregor held out his hand with a grin. Christian kicked him violently beneath the table, and Gregor rose and controlled his grin to a smile.

"I'm glad to meet you, Joe," he said. "Glad to meet any of your friends, too. What can I do for you?"

"Do for me?" crowed the boy. "Lemme sit one second in the saddle on Parade! By Jiminy, would you let me do that?"

"Tomorrow," said Gregor. "Tomorrow morning, wherever you see me and Parade together."

The boy went off in a trance of joy, and Christian said:

"That was all right, but wipe the grin off. Don't look as though you'd just been elected mayor of the town."

Gregor said, in a voice that shuddered with ecstasy: "I could have more than that. I could be the mayor of the town and I could have the ground that it's built on, too. I'm Jim Silver."

Christian smiled at him with narrowed eyes. "Keep on thinking it," he said, "and Heaven help you if you bump into the real man again!"

They turned in early that night. It was a hard job to get across the lobby, for the editor of the newspaper had come to interview the great visitor and get his first impressions of Crow's Nest. And the manager of the big hotel at the spring had come, also, to offer to Jim Silver the best suite in the building. Then there were prominent men from the lumber camps, from the mines, and from the ranches, who wanted to shake hands with Jim Silver.

Gregor shook hands willingly enough, and he smiled on them all before he managed to get to the stairs. There Christian covered his retreat, saying:

"The chiefs all fagged out. He's going to turn in, boys. And you know how it is—he won't take something for nothing, and he doesn't like a lot of publicity. I'll just tell you all one thing. He likes Crow's Nest better than any town he was ever in in his life before. I don't know but what he'll want to settle down in it. He says that a man has to settle down sometime in his days."

They gave the name of Jim Silver a good, hearty cheer, when they heard this announcement, and Christian went up to the room where Gregor was waiting and found him stretched out on the bed with his hands folded under his head, full of gloomy reflections.

"Listen to 'em, Christian! Listen to 'em yell and cheer. All for Jim Silver. Doggone me if it don't make me sort of sick. What's Jim Silver done to get all that glory?"

"Nothing much," said Christian coldly. "You could do the same thing. All you have to do is to shoot straighter than anybody else, ride a horse that can catch anything else on the range, and be willing to lay down your life for a square deal wherever you find the crooks collected. That's all you need to do, and after a few years, if you're not dead and have a lot of luck, you'll be just as famous as Jim Silver."

Gregor stared up at the ceiling.

"I'll tell you what, Barry," he said, "it kind of makes a man think. It kind of makes a man wanta start all over again and try to do the right thing."

"And get buried in the dust that the successful crooks raise as they ride past you? Is that what you want?" asked Christian.

Gregor shook his head and sighed again. "I know," he said. "Only a fellow can't help thinking!"

"You do your thinking in your sleep," said Christian. "While we're on this lay, I intend to do your daytime thinking for you. Keep that straight in your head all the time."

"I'll keep it straight," groaned Gregor.

In the morning, five minutes after the doors of the Merchants & Miners Bank had been opened, Duff Gregor, alias Jim Silver, walked into the institution.

He went alone, but only because Barry Christian had been at work since shortly after daybreak, schooling him in deportment, watching him walk up and down, cursing him for the manner in which he was apt to break into grins and bad English.

Gregor was already more than a little weary, but he was very determined, because he knew all about the greatness of the stakes that he was playing for.

The Merchants & Miners Bank had been reared from a weak infancy to great strength by the skill and the business integrity of a real financier, Henry Wilbur. He had come out to this country and settled in it because he liked it. And the reason he liked it had nothing to do with the sunsets behind towering mountains, but a great deal to do with the splendid forests of pine and spruce that covered the sides of the slopes. He did not wax enthusiastic about the many-colored cliffs of granite and porphyry, but he had a keen eye for the precious metals that could be found veining them here and there. He never brooded dreamily over the pleasant green meadows, but he knew to a half acre how much land was required to keep a steer in good flesh through any sort of a season.

Henry Wilbur knew a great deal about three important industries, but he lacked the intimate practical knowledge which would enable him to step directly into any one of the three fields. He did the next best thing. He picked out men who did have the practical knowledge and training and he backed them. That was how he made money. He was the partner, ready at hand, of any man with brains and industry.

Many a story was told of fellows who had walked into the office of Henry Wilbur without a cent in their pockets and nothing but ideas in their heads, and of how they had came out again with enough gold to break the back of a mule. Sometimes Wilbur put a bet on the wrong man. In those cases, he swallowed his losses with a smile. His faith in human nature could never be destroyed, and since he had both faith and judgment, he won two times out of three, which is enough to make a fortune keep mounting.

He succeeded, in short, because he knew men and because men knew him. They knew that he was loyal, generous, and faithful. They opened their hearts to Henry Wilbur, and he knew how to bolster weak places and reenforce strong points. His bank was like a great heart which kept money, life, hope, and energy constantly in circulation through those mountains. One thing he had never touched was the exploitation of the mineral springs of Crow's Nest. He would have nothing to do with them because he was not assured that there was something more in the cure than faith and advertising. His interests were all based on the soil and its products, vegetable or mineral.

Being a modest man, he had kept the physical surroundings of his bank modest, also. It was simply a little squat house built of natural stone such as cropped out in every vacant lot in Crow's Nest. The stone that had been cleared, years ago, to give a place for the building was what had been used to erect its walls. That was typical of the sensible thrift of Henry Wilbur. He said, when other business men of the growing town urged him to put up a building more in proportion to the size of his success:

"All a man needs is good light to see by, good air to breathe, and space enough to sit and think. I have all these things in this place, and so have the men who work with me. Why should I make a change?"

So he sat in the same office which had been his for twenty years, and behind the very same desk. That desk had begun to spring in the knees, and, therefore, he had remedied the defect by having a long iron rod run through it from side to side. When the nut was screwed up tight on the strong threads, the desk pulled its feet in and was as strong as ever.

It was the sign, "Henry Wilbur, Private Office," that caught the eye of Duff Gregor, as he walked into the bank that morning.

The janitor-doorman, with his eyes popping out from his head, came hurrying to meet Gregor. Behind their clouded windows or in their cages of bronze-gilt steel, the clerks and tellers stood up and gaped at the great man.

Gregor took off his hat and looked slowly around him. "Well, well," he said. "This is what a bank is like, eh? It's about the first time I ever was in one."

He had composed that speech on the way to the bank, because Barry Christian, before sending him off alone, had said: "Don't try to be smart. Jim Silver is so simple that he'd be willing to ask questions of a five-year-old child. There's no side to him, and when he hears a compliment, you can see that it hurts."

The janitor said: "It's a bank, all right. I'll show you over the place, Mr. Silver. Wait just a minute while I get my keys and—"

"Don't you trouble yourself," said Gregor. "The fact is that I'd like to speak a word to Mr. Henry Wilbur, if he's not too mighty busy."

"Mr. Wilbur won't be too busy to see you," said the janitor heartily. "I guess there's nobody on this side of the Mississippi that would be too busy to see you. As soon as Mr. Wilbur comes in, he'll—Hi! Here he comes now with his daughter."

Gregor saw a big man, whose shoulders sloped a bit from too much sitting at a desk, a big man leaning with the weight of his body, a large, flushed face, with dark eyebrows that gave accent to the noble largeness of the forehead. His eyes were grave, his mouth was smiling, and he had the air of one who has faced trouble many times and never with a subdued spirit.

The girl beside him was like her father, but with all the grossness of flesh and the hardness of experience removed. She was slender, straight; she had the direct eye that goes with a simple mind, and that clear and unstained brightness which cannot be after life has been tasted. She was not beautiful. She was something more. Even Gregor could realize that. He wondered what the name of Jim Silver would do to her.

The janitor-doorman was making straight for Henry Wilbur, exclaiming as he came up to him: "Jim Silver is here, Mr. Wilbur. He wants to see you. Here's Mr. Wilbur, Jim Silver!"

Then he added: "Miss Ruth Wilbur too."

Duff Gregor took off his hat so that he could show both courtesy and those two spots of gray hair which Christian had, with such care, arranged about his temple. The banker took off his hat, also. He stood up straight. There was an actual reverence in his voice, as he said: "Mr. Silver, this is a proud and happy moment!"

Even if his glory was vicarious, it was the great instant in the life of Duff Gregor.

CHAPTER 8

The Value of a Name

The girl was blushing and smiling and yet looking Gregor straight in the eye in a confidential sort of way, as though she were not in the least ashamed of showing her admiration. She took his hand and gave it a good hard grip also. She said: "How happy, happy I am to see you, Jim Silver."

Well, that is the way that little children walk up to a big Newfoundland, a picture-book dog, and hang onto its shaggy sides, and throttle it with the grip of their arms, and laugh fearlessly because they know that no harm will come to them. Their trust is perfect. So was the trust which people gave to the name of Jim Silver. And the wretched heart of Duff Gregor suddenly shrank in him and distilled a poison of envy and malice.

He did not have to struggle to keep from grinning; he had to struggle to smile at all. He told Mr. Wilbur that he would like to talk with him for a few moments, and Wilbur took him instantly by the arm toward his private office. The girl was turning to go home. Over her shoulder she was calling out that there was a batch of trout for lunch, if Jim Silver cared to come to the house and eat with them.

Gregor could only smile and shake his head, then he was seated with Wilbur in the sanctum. The banker pulled open a drawer and got out a box of cigars. No, Gregor did not smoke them. He rolled a cigarette of fine tobacco, because that was the only thing that the real Jim Silver was known to smoke.

Wilbur was saying: "Every honest man feels safer when you're near by, Silver. I'm very glad you're here, but I'm also a little worried because I know you generally are on the trail of some rascal or other. I hope it's no big trouble that's brought you to Crow's Nest?"

"The biggest trouble in the world," said Gregor. "Mr. Wilbur, I'm trying to settle down." He paused. Wilbur, listening, with his head canted to one side, nodded a little. He lighted a cigar. As he puffed, he never moved his respectfully attentive eyes from the face of his guest. He waited for the idea to be developed.

Gregor went through with the speech which Christian had composed and which he had carefully rehearsed.

"I've had a good deal of the open trail, and a fellow can get tired."

"Everybody knows you've covered enough trail," said Wilbur.

"After all, I'm getting no younger, and in the winter the old wounds ache. I have a few wounds, Mr. Wilbur, and they touch me up when a norther blows."

"If you had a thousand for every scar, you'd be a rich man, Silver. I know that," he said. Gregor waved the number of his scars aside. He said: "I've decided that I'll stop hunting for trouble and wait for trouble to hunt me, and that's why I came here. I'd heard a good deal about Crow's Nest. It looks like the right sort of a place for me. There's plenty of clean air, and when I came to the town, I wondered what sort of a job I could find, because I'm almost broke."

Wilbur nodded and answered: "I know. You've made half a dozen fortunes and always you've thrown them away again. I understand that, Silver. Every hand that's held out to you, you fill. Now do you mean that you want me to find you a job?"

"That's the idea," said Gregor. "I thought you could give me a steer."

"You could have anything you want," said the banker. "Any rancher would be glad to have you as a foreman, not because you know anything about raising cattle, but because the best cowpunchers on the range would come swarming to work under you. Any miner would be glad to have you as a foreman of his mine, or a superintendent, for the same reason. There will probably be no labor troubles wherever you choose to take charge. And as a matter of fact, if you care to lead a lazy life, you could be the lightning rod in this bank."

"I could be what?" asked Gregor, pretending that he had not understood.

"I mean to say," said the other, "that you could be our watchman—or armed secretary, or sergeant-at-arms, or any other title that you choose to give it. And the minute that it's known that you are here in charge, every man in the mountains will rush to get his money deposited in my bank. There are plenty of old-timers with fortunes tucked away in secret places because they feel that there's no safe in the world that can't be cracked. But there's not a one of them who doesn't feel that Jim Silver can be trusted much further than any amount of armor plate."

The idea began to grow in the mind of the banker. He got up and took a step or two up and down the room, waving his cigar.

"It would be one of the best things that ever happened to this bank, Jim Silver, if we could attach you. Your name would attract a whole crowd of depositors. Many another bank will suffer because you've chosen to appear in Crow's Nest, if you care to work for me. But how do you feel about it?"

"I don't know," said Gregor, staring down at the floor to conceal his exultation, for this was the very manner in which Christian had said that the fish would rise to the bait. "I've never thought of sitting still, with nothing on my mind but hair, as you might say. It would seem a little strange, Mr. Wilbur."

"It would be more than sitting still," declared the banker. "Every one of our new depositors would want to meet you. Every one of them would feel a lot safer about his money after knowing that he had shaken hands with the real Jim Silver. Then, you would want to keep an eye on people who might walk into the bank and plan a holdup. Those things happen, and with your experience, you know a great number of the crooks throughout the West. No, you'd be busy enough, Jim Silver. You'd be a vast asset to us. Yes, I can foresee that you'd bring in added deposits of hundreds of thousands in a year. By thunder, I might change the name of the place and call it the Jim Silver Bank. Your name would stand for bedrock and Gibraltar with every man on the range!"

His excitement grew.

"I'll be able to pay you a hundred a week just as a starter, Mr. Silver, and more than that as soon as my hopes materialize."

The heart of Duff Gregor leaped, but he remembered the careful instructions of Barry Christian, which had been repeated over and over again. Gregor had a feeling that if he went counter to those instructions, Barry Christian would simply kill him out of hand.

So he answered now, instead of swallowing the bait: "If I'm going to be a watchman, I'll only want a watchman's salary. If you'll give me twelve or fifteen dollars a week, that will be enough. If you could put on my old friend, Thomas Bennett, as night watchman, say, at the same figure, I wouldn't ask any more. It's a good thing to have a friend—an old friend in a new town, you know."

"Twelve or fifteen a week!" exclaimed Wilbur. "Why, of course, we'll take on your man. We'll take on anybody you want, but I'd be ashamed to pay Jim Silver, or even a friend of his, as little as that."

Gregor shook his head. "I've got only two eyes; I'm not more honest than a lot of other watchmen, and I can't be worth more pay. Besides, all I need is enough food to eat, and I like my chuck plain. And a couple of beers on Saturday night are enough for me. It isn't a big salary that I'm looking for. It's simply a chance to be quiet, Mr. Wilbur. "

"You'll have that chance, then," said the banker. He was flushed with excitement. "I'm going to spread the news as fast as hard riders can take it through the mountains," he said. "Wait here a moment, Mr. Silver. I'll be back. I've got to have the messages started at once, because there is going to be a golden tide started toward my bank, before the world is a day older."

He hurried out and was gone for a few moments. When he came back, he was fairly laughing with happiness.

"A dozen men will be hitting the trail with their mustangs inside an hour," he said, "and every place on the range will have the news inside of a week. After that, the golden flood begins. And you tell me that I can only give you the wages of an ordinary cowpuncher? It's not fair, Silver!"

"It's fair to me," said Gregor. "Enough is as good as a bale of hay. Let it go at that."

"We can argue it over later on," answered Wilbur. "Now we'll look over the bank."

He took out a bunch of keyes and led the way straight to the great safe. It was the one modern feature of the bank, and Gregor looked it over with understanding and rather despairing eyes. This was certainly no job for a "can opener." This was a case where "soup" would have to be used.

He photographed that safe with a careful eye and then followed the president of the bank down into the cellar storage rooms, and up again through the main floor, and into the attic.

Wilbur said: "Your job begins this minute, if you want it to."

"I'd better find a shack," said Gregor. "The best thing for me would be to find a shack where Bennett and I can live; we'll move out of the hotel and get into quarters where we can cook for ourselves. Thank you, Mr. Wilbur. I hope I can be half as useful as you think."

CHAPTER 9

A Chance Meeting

Far north of Crow's Nest, the real Jim Silver came through the mottled and ghostly pallor of a birch wood and stopped at the edge of a stream. It was a silent little creek that seemed to steal along with a finger pressed against its lips. The sun streaked down through the trees and glinted like metal on the thousand upturned edges of the curling bark. That bark was thin as paper. It had a yellow tint in its white, and by that "Arizona Jim" knew it to be the yellow birch. He picked off a leaf. The stem was fuzzy, the leaf coarser and more serrated of edge than the black birch.

Jim Silver looked up from the water and the trunks of the trees to the lift of the thin branches that seemed to him to be bursting upward and outward, like green fountains. Life rushed up from the ground through those curving lines that never returned to the earth again. Happiness rushed up through the heart of Jim Silver, also.

He was most of his time among the grays of the desert, the blues and browns of the great mountains, or the perpetual twilight of pine and spruce forests. As he stood in this delicate woodland, he wondered why he did not give more of his life to such surroundings. It was not silent, really. Whenever the wind stirred, it seemed as though an invisible river were streaming across the heavens. And even when the wind did not move, there was always a stealthy approaching noise, though at first this was

58

not audible to ears more attuned to the sounds of the deserts and the iron mountains.

The stallion stood as quietly as his master. He would have liked to try the taste of some of the tender shoots of the saplings, but the whole air of Jim Silver was one of caution, and, therefore, the horse stood on guard with shining eyes. It was he that gave warning of a possible danger by tossing his head and looking fixedly up the stream. A moment later a canoe slid around the sharp angle of the bend. Silver could hear the gurgling of the water as the paddle blade was driven into it with a short, powerful side stroke, to straighten out the little bark canoe.

He wondered if the bearded man in the canoe would see him. He stood still, without a word. The paddler worked with leisurely strokes. He seemed to have time for nothing except watching the intricacies of the current, which was full of shiftings in spite of its soundless flow, and yet when he was at a little distance, he called out suddenly, and backed water.

He grounded the canoe and sprang out. No wonder he had seen the man on the bank, for it seemed to Silver that he had never seen brighter, smaller eyes, more like those of a bird. They were buried deeply in the hairy face. He came striding up the bank with his hand out, a big, burly fellow, laughing with pleasure.

"Hey, Jim Silver!" he cried. "You taking a vacation out of Crow's Nest? Don't go and tell me that you been and given up your job down there, or I'll tell 'em to fetch my money back to my old bank!"

Silver looked at him with a quiet concern as he shook hands. "I take a vacation once in a while," he said.

"And you're goin' back, eh?" asked the stranger. "When I heard that Jim Silver had taken a job in the Merchants & Miners Bank that old Henry Wilbur runs, I decided that that was the place for my coin. I ain't got much, but every thousand looks as big as a whale to a fellow like me. And I says to myself, where would my money rest as safe as in a bank that Jim Silver is around? The minute I heard the news, I made the change—and then, doggone my spots, I find you up here lookin' at the runnin' of the creek a whole day's ride from Craw's Nest. Yeah, a whole day, even for Parade!"

He held out his hand toward the muzzle of the stallion, which laid back threatening ears.

The fellow laughed. "I clean forgot that Parade is likely to be poison to strangers. What we know about Jim Silver makes a gent feel that even his guns and hosses can't do nothin' except what's right!"

He was full of talk, bubbling with it, yet Jim Silver did not know his name when he stepped again into the canoe and sped it down the stream with long, powerful strokes of the paddle. A twist of the bank took him out of sight, and yet Silver remained there staring at the empty corner of the creek and seeing his own thoughts.

He was beginning to grow more and more discontented with certain features of his life. He had tried for years to avoid the world, but the world was continually thrusting itself upon him. It was typical that in the rush and pause of existence among these trees he should be rudely given a message that made him turn back on his trail and speed toward Crow's Nest.

He had never been in that town; he never had wanted to be in such a crowded place if he could avoid it; but when he learned that "Jim Silver" was working there for a bank, he was alarmed. Nobody could be wearing his name by chance; he could be sure that there was only one "Jim Silver" for everyone on the range. Some rascal, then, had tried to assume his identity.

He wondered why he had not explained to this unknown man that he had never worked in Crow's Nest, but his whole nature was against talk and in favor of action.

Whatever scheme the fellow in Crow's Nest might have in mind, a vague alarm from a distance would merely serve to frighten him away. And, since the real Jim Silver was only a day from the town, it would be better for him to turn up on the spot and confront the crook face to face.

It was the sort of danger which he had never conceived. He had been in peril of his life more times than he could count, but hitherto no one had endangered his good name. He turned out of that wood, pulled up the cinches a little tighter, and mounted Parade. The stallion was in perfect trim and ready for a good run. He would have need of all his endurance before his master was through with him this day. The night would pour over the mountains, it would be early the next morning before Jim Silver could possibly reach Crow's Nest.

He looked toward the west and saw that the falling sun already was gathering about it a bright halo of the horizon mist. Then he picked up his course, named to his mind's eye the landmarks which he must follow by day and night, and loosed the reins of Parade.

It was only a little later than this moment that big Duff Gregor, walking with Ruth Wilbur in the garden behind her father's house, entirely lost control of himself and "went wrong."

There were two troubles in the situation. One was that Duff Gregor was convinced that he had a "way with women"; the other trouble was that the girl had treated him like a brother. Then the garden was more of a forest than its name indicated, and as the sun slanted to the west and the rose and gold of it washed among the trees, Gregor was carried off his feet and away by a stream of romance.

Ruth had run her hand through the crook of his arm, and side by side they wandered up and down, the girl talking and laughing, and the man growing more and more dizzy.

For one thing, he was glad to be away from the continual surveillance of Barry Christian. For Barry had made him swear to confine himself to the little shack which they had rented on a back alley of the town. Unless Gregor were actually in the bank, he had given his word that he would be in the small house. This day he had broken his promise—and he was unspeakably glad of it.

He began to see other possibilities of the future. If he were to double-cross Barry Christian, he would be in danger from that outlaw's guns; but, on the other hand, if he married Ruth Wilbur, he would be on the direct road toward a fortune.

That was as far as he thought out the problem. He was not doing much thinking, just then. Suddenly, turning on the girl, he stammered out a few confused words and grabbed her in his arms and kissed her, not taking time to note the sudden revulsion of feeling in her eyes.

She made no outcry. She simply stood like a stone. And then came what seemed the most hateful voice in the world, saying: "Jim! Are you crazy?"

It was Barry Christian, suddenly appearing from among the trees by a small side path.

Gregor stepped back from the girl far enough to get a bit of perspective in the mind as well as the eye, and he saw that he had made something more than a fool of himself. She had a handkerchief pressed against her mouth, and she was looking at him as though he were a monster out of a strange world.

He tried to say something more, but as Christian came up the path, the courage and the wits of Gregor both deserted him. He turned and bolted through the brush and got away from those fixed and nightmare eyes of fear. No, he decided that it was not fear so much as disgust.

That was what kept the cold shudders going up and down his back. She was more horrified than angered or frightened. He would not have minded anger or fear, he thought.

In the meantime, Barry Christian, coming up the path, had seen how the girl bowed her head and stared down at the ground. She was obviously trying to put together her former ideas of "Jim Silver" and the reality as she had found it.

Christian took off his hat. "Miss Wilbur," he said, "doggone me if it ain't the meanest moment in my life. Not this here moment, but having seen Jim Silver act like that. I wanta say something to you, and I hope you believe it."

She raised her head, but still she seemed to be seeing her own ideas more than the face of Christian.

"I simply don't believe it," she said. "I don't believe that it was Jim Silver."

"What?" cried Christian, thoroughly knocked off balance. "You don't believe that it's really Jim Silver?"

"He's not the man I've been hearing about for all these years," said the girl. "The man I've heard about couldn't act like that."

"It's because he don't know how to deal with a girl," said Christian. "You know how it is. He ain't the sort that ever has to do with women. He never pays no attention to them. I might 'a' knowed the other day that he was clean out of his head about you, because he talked for hours. He talked, and he said that he'd never seen anybody like you. He talked like you were an angel out of heaven. He's out of his head about you, that's what the matter is. Ma'am, you'd do him a pile of harm if you talk about this."

"Harm him?" she said, throwing up her head in a fine way. "I'd rather cut off my hand. Perhaps you're right, and it's simply that he doesn't understand. But to turn into a brute—" She checked herself sharply and added: "It would be a pitiful sort of a world if Jim Silver couldn't be forgiven. He's done enough glorious things for a few bad ones to be forgotten. Will you tell him that I won't speak a single word about this to my father, or to anybody else?"

"Ma'am," said Barry Christian, really moved, "I suppose that I should 'a' sort of expected this kind of talk from the daughter of a man like Henry Wilbur. It'd be the ruin of Silver if people got an idea that he was out of his head about women. Ma'am, he's the sort of a man that's never done wrong, and if once folks find out that he ain't perfect, they'll never forgive themselves for ever praising him."

She shook her head.

"Tell him that I won't talk," she said. "It's nothing so dreadful—the kissing of a girl." Her lip curled. "I hope that I'll never have to see his face again; if I do I'll manage to endure it. That's all."

"I want to say," said Christian, "that poor Jim Silver—" She lifted a hand.

"You can't say a thing about Jim Silver that I haven't thought all by myself," she told him. "I've lain awake at night and wondered how there could be such a man in the world. Well—now I'm a little sick and I don't want to think about him any more. Good evening, Mr. Bennett."

That was the best that Barry Christian could do, and he left the banker's place and went straight across Crow's Nest to the shack. There was still a little time before he went on duty, and after the end of his partner's daytime regime.

The shack stood on the edge of a gully that split across the face of the mountain town. Sometimes, after a rain, there was a great racket of water dashing among the big stones in the bottom of the ravine, but as a rule the gulch was empty, and the little shack stood on the verge of its crumbling slope. It was not worth moving, and it was, after almost any heavy storm, apt to slide down to ruin in the bottom of the canyon.

In the house Christian found Duff Gregor walking up and down with long strides. The sun was resting its rim on the edge of the world and pouring flame across the mountains, and Barry Christian wished that real fire might rush out on Gregor and consume him. But he said nothing. He simply stood in the doorway and watched the promenade of Gregor, until the latter whirled about.

"All right! Go ahead and shout it out!" said Gregor. "Tell me I'm a fool."

Christian said nothing.

"How could I know that she was that way?" demanded Gregor. "I can't understand a girl like that. Had her arm in mine. She *put* her arm in mine. Laughin' like a fool, she was, most of the time. Laughin', and turnin' her eyes up to mine and shinin' them at me. How could I tell what she was like? A girl that acts like that—that's different!"

Still Christian was silent, until Gregor broke down and begged: "What did she say?"

"After you turned around and ran like a kicked dog?" said Christian. "Why, I talked to her and made a good many excuses. I said that you weren't used to women. I said a good many other things. Finally, she told me that you were just a brute."

"Brute?" shouted Gregor, rising to his toes with wrath.

"Just a low brute," said Christian, "not worthy of a thought."

"She said that about Jim Silver, did she?" roared Gregor. "After the things that I've done for the world and—"

"What have you done for the world, Gregor?" asked Christian.

Gregor cleared his throat. "I got sort of tangled up just then," he admitted. "I mean, for all she knows, I'm Jim Silver, and yet she'd throw me out of the door like that. Just for kissing her, eh? That shows what she's made of. That shows she ain't no good. I wouldn't have a gross of her for a gift. She ain't worth a—"

"Shut up," said Christian.

"I won't shut up," cried Gregor. "I'm goin' to—"

"Shut up or I'll shut you up," said Christian. "I've half a mind to cut the heart out of you, and partly because you have the crust to talk like that about Ruth Wilbur. Why, Gregor, it soils the mind of a girl like that to so much as think down to you. But as a matter of fact, she's not going to say a word to her father—and so you've still got the job. Be thankful for that!"

"She told you she wouldn't speak to him?" exclaimed Gregor.

"Yes."

Gregor fell into a chair and mopped his face. "I thought it was the finish of everything!" he gasped at last. "I thought the big chance was queered. I thought it was the end."

"It is the end," answered the other.

"What d'you mean?" "This is the night, Duff."

"You mean for crackin' the safe?"

"This is the night."

Gregor came bounding to his feet again.

"Don't talk like a fool, Barry!" he argued. "Every day they're bringin' in money by the carload. The little one-horse banks all through the mountains are being cleaned out, and the depositors are sendin' us their money. They must be gettin' in thousands of dollars every day over there in Wilbur's bank. The old man smiles like a risin' sun every day. Barry, if we make our clean-up and jump now, we're missin' a lot of cream."

Christian nodded. "I intended to wait for another week," he declared, "in the hope that we would be safe that long—before Jim Silver hears that there's an alias of his down here in Crow's Nest. But after you've made this break, I'm on edge to get the job finished and over with."

"Why?" asked Gregor. "As long as she'll keep her mouth shut, why shouldn't we wait? Another week might bring in a lot more cash into that little bank. It's bulgin' now. Barry, it's goin' to be sweet pickin's! The sweetest pickin's you ever knew, and I'm not foolin'!"

He threw up his hands. He was trembling like flame with his excitement.

"We can quit the game. I'm goin' to Europe and settle down and have a rest. I'm goin' to taste some life!" cried Duff Gregor. "And every day we wait before we pull the job, the better for us. Besides, we ain't got the combination, yet."

He waited, panting, resting much on the last remark he had made.

"I think I have that combination," said Christian. "The other day I found a chance to be alone with that safe and I took off the dial knob of the lock and put a bit of steel wire—no use explaining the details—on the inside surface of the dial. I replaced the knob, and I think that bit of wire may be able to tell me the right combination."

"You're a fox!" exclaimed Gregor in great admiration. Then he added: "But it's all the more reason why we ought to wait till the last minute—"

Something in the face of Christian stopped him, and he asked: "What's the matter, Barry? You look gray as a stone."

"I don't know what it is," answered Christian. "In a woman you'd call it premonition, or instinct. I don't know what it is in me, but it's a thing that tells me we haven't much time to spare. Tonight's the night. You start cooking the dynamite now and make the soup."

"Soup?" said Gregor nervously. "But what's the matter? I thought you said that you would be able to read the combination?"

"Perhaps I will. If we had time to leave the wire inside the lock for another day, I'm sure I could. But if I fail, we'll have to try to blow the safe." The other closed his eyes and groaned.

Christian came up to him and took him by the lapels of his coat. "Listen to me!" he said.

"I'm listenin'," groaned Duff Gregor.

"If you lose your nerve like a dog, I'll have one bit of satisfaction before I leave this town. I'll cut your throat for you, Gregor!"

Gregor, staring at him, knew there was nothing that Barry Christian could have said that he could have meant more thoroughly.

"You think I'd welsh on you?" said Gregor. "Wait till the pinch comes before you start yowlin' about me. Do your own job as well as I do mine, and we'll walk off with the inside linin' of that safe, I tell you!"

"All right," said Christian. "Be a man. That's all I ask of you. Get the soup ready and work up some of that yellow laundry soap till it's the right consistency for the running of a mold. You know how to do that?"

"I know," Gregor nodded. "Only—it's bad business in a place like this. In a business district in a big town, where everybody's asleep in the middle of the night, it's not so bad. But the noise of shooting a safe will get a hundred people on horseback, in a place like this!" Christian turned in the doorway, regarded his companion silently for a moment, and then, without another word, walked off in the direction of the bank, for it was time for him to take up his duties as night watchman.

CHAPTER 10

Gregor's Preparations

There is a certain amount of care necessary when dynamite is converted into "soup," because when the sediment has settled to the bottom of the pot, there remains a rather muddy liquid which can be strained off, and this is almost pure nitroglycerin. And nitroglycerin has to be handled with awe, because if it is bottled up under too tight a stopper, it is likely to oppress itself with its own evaporation, and explode. And if it grows too cold, it is likely to explode, also. Of course, sudden jerks and jars are apt to be fatal too. And when Duff Gregor had finished making the soup, he was in a sweat.

For one thing, he had locked the doors of the shack, and the night was warmer than usual. But he could not permit his usual audience of admiring small boys and youths of the town to assemble and watch this extraordinary cookery of his. When they came, and knocked and called to him, he simply had to tell them that he was out of sorts. They went off reluctantly and left him to his work.

He got the laundry soap prepared also, mashing it up and moistening it just enough to give it the consistency of a very strong, tough, and sticky mortar. He had a length of fine wire, too, which could be used in running the mold just over the meager crack which outlined the door of the safe.

When he had finished these preparations, he paused in some doubt. He was so accustomed to working according to the direct

69

orders of Christian that he was hardly prepared to use his own initiative. But he knew that the contemptuous silence of Christian's departure had been a direct challenge to him and his efficiency. Therefore, he remembered that they must have their horses ready. They had the chestnut stallion, of course. Every evening he had been in the habit of riding the frisky horse out for exercise, taking ways where he would not be observed, because it was certain that he could not control the chestnut in an emergency in the same way that the real Parade was handled by Jim Silver.

He got the stallion ready and he also saddled the plain-looking mare which Christian had provided for himself. This animal had prominent hip bones, carried its head low, and had a very ugly head. But the mare was in reality a good piece of running machinery and in a pinch would probably give as good an account of itself as the more showy stallion.

Then Gregor cleaned a pair of Winchester rifles and prepared in two saddlebags sufficient provisions to keep a man alive for a week if he were careful in his diet. A blanket and a slicker were all the additional weight that he dared to incorporate in each pack, because if they had to blow the safe and the noise were heard, they'd have to travel fast.

Last of all, he got two canvas bags, the mouths of which could be closed with drawstrings. They had been prepared long before, and they were to hold the "inside lining" of the Merchants & Miners Bank. When these had been folded under his arm, he looked at his clock and saw that it was getting on toward midnight. It was too early, he decided. It was not the time of night when Christian would want to make the attempt, because there were still too many people about the town.

He lay down, intending to count the minutes, but he awakened with a terribly guilty start to find it was two-thirty, and the flame flickering in the lamp, as the oil was nearly exhausted.

That reminded him of the dark lantern. He filled it from the oil can with kerosene, made sure that the shutter was well greased so that it would make no sound no matter how quickly it was opened and shut, and then he set out.

If midnight had been too early, he felt that this hour was too late. Dawn came early at this season of the year—extra early, he always felt, among the mountains, and it would be nearly three o'clock before he arrived at the bank!

In the meantime, what if the girl's emotions had got the better of her promise and induced her to speak to her father about his conduct? What if his suspicions had been aroused? What if he had come to doubt the integrity of his two watchmen? What if he had decided to post a second and secret guard for the watching of the bank, this night? It seemed possible, it seemed probable. It grew to a near certainty in the brain of Gregor before he finally had finished leading the horses up the gulch and had taken them from the edge of it to a group of young saplings that stood behind the bank

It was an excellent line of retreat to leave the bank, get the horses, and then depart from town by riding up the gulch. It was an excellent line unless they were pursued. In that case, they would have to take the straightest line, right through the main streets. The hair prickled on the head of Gregor as he thought of that possibility.

He finished tethering the horses and stepped out into the open night. The bank was right before him, looking squat and strong as a fort. He had never realized that it was so large. He scanned the ground on all sides of it and saw nothing. There was a vacant lot on one side of it, and beyond the lot stood a boarding house, now silent and with unlighted windows. But the stars glimmered faintly on the black panes. The boarding house was as dangerous as could be; it was filled with young workingmen and was sure to have plenty of guns of all sorts in it. Young men sleep like wildcats. The least sound is enough to rouse them.

Duff Gregor himself felt twice as old as his twenty-eight years.

On the other side of the bank there was a drygoods shop. The man and woman who ran it lived in a back room of the shop, but they would be fairly harmless, Gregor thought. "Dutch Charlie," the proprietor, was a red-faced, fat old man with a waddling step. He had not the look of a fighter, but in the West one cannot tell. The mildest "worm" may bite like a rattlesnake.

Gregor, when he had finished this quick survey, went slowly on, stepping softly. He wished, now, that he had the quiet, natural stride of a fellow like Christian, to say nothing of that ghostly footfall of Taxi. There was Taxi to be thought of, in the immediate future, because he knew that when the bank job had ended, Christian would not fail to call in at the shack of Taxi and try to put him out of the way.

Sometimes, when Gregor heard Christian talk, it seemed to him that the great criminal hated Taxi more than he hated Jim Silver himself. And for a good reason. Taxi was an out-and-out crook who had learned to go "straight," owing to the influence of Silver. And there is nothing that a criminal forgives less easily than virtue in one of his own kind.

Down the eastern side of the bank, Gregor saw nothing, but when he was halfway along the wall, he was aware of something stealing up behind him. His brain spun. He felt sick in the pit of his stomach, and then, as he whirled with a gun in his hand, he saw, dimly against the starlight, the welcome and familiar outline of the head and shoulders of big Barry Christian.

Christian came up to him and said: "All right, Duff. It's only me. You can be thankful that you didn't pull the gun on a stranger."

Gregor felt mutely rebellious, but this was not a time for argument. With a clear foresight, he understood that, if he lived a thousand years in league with Christian, he would never be able to be entirely in the right. Something in him was lacking. Or did Christian merely carp?

They paused at the side door of the bank. Christian took out his bunch of keys, opened the door, and led the way inside, saying casually: "It'll have to be the soup, brother. I've tried to work the combination already, but the wire trick hasn't worked. It hasn't been in the lock long enough to register the numbers for me."

He spoke, it seemed to Duff Gregor, loudly enough to call the attention of everyone in the town. And already, in imagination, Gregor saw the streets filled with people hurrying toward the noise in the bank.

CHAPTER 11

Safe Cracking

The greatest difficulty to be faced, once they started to work, was that a night lamp burned constantly inside the bank, and through the plate glass windows any passer-by along the street could see nearly every detail of what happened inside the big room. As a matter of fact, people who returned home late at night were very apt to pause and glance through the windows at the forest of bronze-gilt bars which were all that guarded the door of the safe. Even honest men may contemplate theft to which they would never put their hands.

The first question that Gregor asked was: "How do we keep in the dark here?"

"We don't," said Christian.

He took the two canvas sacks, spread them out, and then hung them against the steel fence that ran between the front of the safe and the street windows.

"This is the best we can do," he said.

"Hold on!" objected Gregor. "Anybody who looks in will be used to seeing the glimmering of the front of the safe! He'll notice the difference when his eye runs into those sacks."

"People usually see what they expect to see, and nothing more," answered Christian.

"But what if somebody comes along and uses his brain?" asked Gregor.

"Every job like this is fifty per cent chance and luck," said Christian. "Would you want the money if it were simply given to you on a platter, Duff? I think better of you than that!"

He seemed to mean what he said. But one never could tell what real thinking went on behind the mask of that smooth, easy voice and gentle intonation.

"Hold a light. Open the shutter about halfway. You seem to have thought of a few of the necessaries," said Christian by way of compliment.

Gregor kneeled and opened the shutter gingerly. In spite of his precautions in greasing the slides, it seemed to him that he heard a faint sound, and he jumped.

"Sorry the thing makes so much noise. I greased it, anyway," said Gregor.

Christian laughed out loud. The sound roared and thundered in the ears of Gregor. He thought, for an instant, that his companion had gone mad.

"We'll make more noise than that, before we're through," said Christian.

He fell to work, straightway, running the mold of yellow laundry soap around the edges of the circular door. He worked rapidly, whistling to himself. Finally, when he had completed his work, he looked it over carefully. When he was certain that all was well—and this seemed to Gregor to have endured for an hour—he started pouring in the "soup."

After that, the preparations went quickly. The fuse was attached. They hurried to a far corner of the big room after the fuse had been lighted by Gregor. There they lay flat on their faces, and Gregor listened to the bumping of his heart and wondered how flesh and blood could withstand such a strain.

Then came the explosion. It was a thick, dull, puffing sound which seemed to be accompanied, as if in the great distance, by a far-off report.

Gregor felt a distinct pressure, as he thought, on his whole body. He was up like a cat, but Christian was ahead of him. They ran into the safe room, and saw that the door of the safe was still fitted snugly in place!

Gregor whirled about with a groan.

"We're beaten! You bungled it! You bungled it like a great fool!" he said, and started to run.

He ran straight into the hard fist of Christian. It bumped half the wits out of his head and deposited him with a solid thump on the floor of the bank.

Staring up with dim, dazed eyes, he wondered, with what was left of his frightened brain, if Christian intended to double-cross him—to turn him over for the attempted job and drop the blame on his shoulders. Then he heard Christian saying calmly:

"Don't run out like a yellow hound till you know the job's a lost job. Look here. The door's been budged a little. It's been budged and settled a shade. This crack on the top of it is a hair broader than the crack at the bottom, now. We can get some soup into that upper crack on the next try and—"

"Next try?" exclaimed Duff Gregor, as he stumbled dizzily to his feet. "Are you goin' to be fool enough to wait here and make another try when—"

"Shut up and get to work," said Christian. "I'd rather walk up Salt Creek with my eyes open than to walk out of this place before I'm driven out. You said one true thing today. There's maybe half a million dollars inside that safe!"

Gregor panted: "But that noise has been heard! We'd only stay here to be found out and—"

"Take that soap, what's left of it, and give me a hand," said the calm bandit. "We have to work faster this time, that's all. And we're sure to win."

Gregor, staring mutely for a moment, was amazed to find himself bending to the task that had been assigned to him. All his volition was urging his heels to scamper away toward freedom, but his physical body he found bending there in front of the safe!

Then came the thing that he had known would happen. There was a murmur of voices, dim and far away as the murmuring of bees. And then a hand shook at the front door of the bank, and succeeded in making it rattle faintly. He turned and stared past the two sacks that partially concealed them, and saw that a dozen people were gathered on the sidewalk, peering through the plate glass into the interior of the bank.

Gregor turned to gasp out: "The sidewalk's full of 'em, but there's still the back door. Quick, Barry! We can get to the horses and run out of town before they tag us with lead, maybe."

Christian caught his arm with a rigid hand.

"Go out there and open the door and send 'em away!" he commanded. "Don't turn rotten and crumble to pieces on me. Remember that you're Jim Silver! Tell 'em anything. Tell 'em that a lamp exploded, but get 'em all out of the bank again. Understand? March, Gregor! I'll keep you covered till you get back to me!"

Mad? Of course he was mad, but he was also armed, and the hand which held the Colt and covered Gregor was as steady as a stone. Duff Gregor did not argue. In another moment it seemed that the mob would break down the front door of the bank. Practically every penny of the savings of the men of Crow's Nest was lodged in the big safe of Henry Wilbur, and the inhabitants would be as tender of the safety of the bank as of their own lives. If that door went down before Gregor had accomplished anything, he had a very strong idea that the cruel devil in front of him would shoot him down before managing an escape.

So Gregor turned without a word and walked toward the door.

He could not believe that he was headed in that direction. He could not believe that he was actually waving to the men beyond the door, covering the sidewalk. He went through the motions like a sleepwalker, and always the cold consciousness of the revolver that watched him nudged him forward.

Then he heard a general outcry: "Jim Silver! It's Jim Silver! There he comes. Everything's all right!"

The sound of those words warmed the freezing soul of Duff Gregor. He threw open the front door of the bank and stood on the threshold.

"Hey, what happened, Jim?" asked half a dozen of them at once. They pressed close. If he gave an inch, they would swarm in a stream into the bank, he knew. Therefore, he stood fast and merely said: "I was fixing the gasoline lamp, and the fool thing went *poom* all at once. It made a terrible racket. I don't wonder that it woke you up. Sorry, boys!"

They began to smile and nod at him. It was a wild-looking crowd. Every man and youngster in the lot had a rifle, a shotgun, or a revolver showing. They had come out ready for business, and they looked the part.

"How come you're on duty at night?" asked one lean, gray, suspicious old fox of a trapper.

"Bennett's a little knocked out," said Duff Gregor, "so I'm staying around. Not that Tom really needs any help, but there's a lot of money in this bank, boys, and I sort of feel that the whole responsibility of watching it is on my shoulders. You know how it is."

"Good old Silver," said one of the men. "We couldn't have the bank better watched if we had ten men on the job day and night."

The crowd began to break up, and Duff Gregor, with amazement, watched them go. It was too simple; it was too easy. Suddenly he was struck with awe for the wisdom of Barry Christian, who had foreseen exactly what would happen.

While still a few lingered, Gregor closed and locked the front door, hearing one of the bystanders remark:

"Suppose that a gent was to break into that there bank and think that he had pretty clear sailing, and suppose that up out of a corner comes Jim Silver at him—wouldn't it be hell on him, eh?"

And they laughed, as Duff Gregor closed that door and shut out their voices to a dimness.

Before he reached the safe room again, the last of the men had scattered from the sidewalk. In front of the safe he found Barry Christian already calmly at work, running the mold with his swift, cunning fingers.

Without looking up from what he was doing, he said: "You did that well, Gregor. You're a man, partner. A real man. And these people of Crow's Nest are real geese. All honest people are fools, or else they wouldn't be honest. Duff, you and I are going to do things together. We may crack a sweeter nut than this, even, one of these days."

Duff Gregor, squinting at the future, was not sure that he wished to remain in partnership with a man like Barry Christian, who was himself fearless and who demanded heroism of all who worked with him. And yet there was a wonderful glory and exhilaration in being with that famous man. The future looked like a storm, but like a golden storm.

He set about working as fast as he could to help Christian. They finished their preparations once more, and the last of the "soup" was poured into the mold. Over the top of the safe door they now battened rugs and carpets in thick masses, and when they had lighted the fuse and retired, there was at last an explosion far more muffled than the first one. Even so, the entire building jarred, and the windows shook and jingled like so many great castanets.

They got up from the floor where they had been lying and ran forward. They saw that the huge door of the safe had swung wide open on its hinges, and, with a cry of joy, Gregor leaped forward and thrust into the inner door the key with which it was always opened. It had not been hard to get that key from its hiding place in the cashier's desk, because no one considered the inner door of the safe of such very great importance. It was important enough now to make the heart of Gregor stand still, because, no matter how he turned and twisted, he could not budge the inner bolt. Then he understood. The force of the explosion which had knocked the outer door open had served to jam, hopelessly, the lock of the inner door!

He turned a desperate face toward Barry Christian, and beyond him he saw the gray of the morning come shimmering through the eastern windows of the bank.

CHAPTER 12

The Loot

Neither of them spoke. Christian made a gesture that forced Gregor to recoil while the chief partner himself took the key and worked with it for an instant. Then, in turn, he stood back, dusted off his hands, and nodded. He whirled on his heel, left the safe room, and it suddenly occurred to Gregor that Christian, in silence, was going to walk off and give up the job.

He was wrong. Christian returned in a moment, bringing with him a small sack of padded canvas, which he laid on the floor and unrolled. It contained a good kit of burglary tools. Christian took out a mallet made of soft iron and a pair of untempered steel wedges, with points drawn down as fine as a pin. He wrapped the head of the mallet in cloth, laid the edge of a wedge against the top crack of the inner door of the safe, and began to tap gently. He tapped with force hardly sufficient to break an egg, then with greater and greater effort until the dull, padded sound of the blows was louder than a drumbeat in the frightened ears of Gregor.

Then Gregor forgot his fears, for he saw that the first wedge had actually entered a little.

Yes, more than that—the wedge was not only entering, but the door was beginning to groan under the strain. If the door could be made to yield the least bit to the first narrow wedge, the second one would soon have an entrance with its greater bevel and weight.

In fact, that door was presently bending like a bow along the upper edge. Two wedges were shifted down the forward face, close to the lock, and driven in side by side. Before the heels of them had disappeared, the lock burst with a sound like a snapping piano wire. The little door came shuddering open, and there appeared before the eyes of Duff Gregor the most beautiful sight in the world—a series of little, bright, polished-steel drawers, each to be opened with its separate key.

But they did not need to pause in order to fit the keys. Having passed the first barriers, these that remained were nothing. With a wedge and a little fine steel crowbar, the expert hands of Barry Christian pried open those drawers rapidly. Into the two capacious canvas sacks, which had already done a different sort of duty on this night, the riches of the mountains began to be dropped, in the form of bonds of all sorts of paper wealth; but most of all, the hearts of the pair were gladdened by the treasure in hard cash.

It would not have been there if a few more weeks had passed. It would have gone into safe forms of investment, of course; but, in the meantime, the sudden jump in prestige which the bank had enjoyed since the arrival of "Jim Silver" had flooded the big safe with quantities of paper money.

That money was snatched out and handed into the sacks. Only one thick packet enchanted the eye and the touch of Duff Gregor that he could not give up to the sack. It was a beautiful, thick sheaf of fifties, almost brand-new, stiff and firm as a board and full half an inch thick. He could not resist passing that wad into his own pocket. He knew that Christian marked him, but that did not matter. It was not the question of stealing the money, but the joy of having it intimately under his fingers and pressing in a lump against his body. He felt not only a richer but a better and more important man. He felt that Fate would not hand out such favors and fortune as this except to a friend.

He had his grasp on the throat of the world, he felt, and the world would have to pay for his hold before he was finished with it.

That was the mind of amiable Gregor as they finished loading the canvas sacks, and, looking out of the window, saw that the gray of the morning was turning to rose.

They got to the back door of the bank, unlocked it, and listened. The town was wakening. The gambling and playing element must still be snoring, and its members would continue to sleep until noon; but the others, the workers, would be up before the sun.

The vacant lot was pearl-gray with dew. As they started for the horses, a boy began to whistle like a lark. They saw him come over the grass in bare, brown feet. He left a double streak of darkness behind him, where he had knocked the moisture off the grass.

Barry Christian turned a bit toward his friend and in a soft but profound voice he cursed that boy and all his forebears.

They tied the bags to the saddles and mounted as the boy came up to them.

"Hey, hullo, Jim," said the youngster. "Whatcha doin' up this time of day? You don't go to work for three, four hours yet. And how come that you ain't back there in the bank, Mr. Bennett?"

He cocked his head on one side and peered at them. He was as bright and keen as a magpie, and just as cruelly mischievous.

"I've got my helper on the job, son," said Barry. He turned his horse.

"Hey, who's your helper?" asked the boy. "Whatcha mean? Who's your helper? I didn't know that you had a helper."

"So long, son!" said Gregor.

They began to jog their horses, but not in the direction up the gulch in which, as Gregor knew, his chief wanted to travel. Instead, Christian was heading straight across the town.

The boy actually came scampering after them. He had a voice as clear and chanting loud as the voice of a rooster—a new, young rooster delighted with his task of rousing the world in the morning.

"Hey, Jim!" he yelled. "Where you goin'? Who's the new man in the bank? How come you both are off work?"

That voice went like a hot needle through and through the brain of Duff Gregor. They turned up the first side alley. A woman was coming in from the woodpile behind the house, her apron filled with wood. She paused and shaded her eyes, looking into the bright east toward those two early travelers.

When she saw Gregor, she actually dropped the wood so that she could clap her hands together, and she shouted:

"Hi, Jim Silver! Go it, Jim! Good luck to ye, boy!"

They passed out of sight of her, and still the shrill voice of the boy was piping in the distance.

"The devil take him! He's started the town on the trail with his yelling," said Christian.

"He'll be back there at the bank, in a minute, and then he'll be pretty sure to look around to see my helper. If he doesn't spy the open door of the safe the first thing, I'll be surprised."

"But why take this direction? I thought you wanted to ride up through the gulch! That's the best way to get out of Crow's Nest. There's regular hole-in-the-wall country behind those hills."

"Because I want to start in a false direction, Duff," said Christian. "We've not finished the hardest part of this job yet."

"Not finished it? Not when we've bamboozled the town and cracked the safe for them? What do you call hard?" said Gregor.

"I call it hard," answered Christian, "to get away from a thousand or so men who have good horses and who know how to shoot straight and who are going to keep on our trail until their feet wear out under them. Gregor, they trusted you as they would have no one else on earth, and when they find we've cheated 'em and that you're gone, those men are going to go practically insane. Believe me, because I know. Every man in Crow's Nest is going to be a bloodhound, and when the news gets out on the range, everybody in the mountains will be gunning for us."

They had cleared the outskirts of Crow's Nest, by this time, and, coming to a narrow, rocky gorge that headed west, Christian at once turned down it.

"You're wasting time and distance," cautioned Gregor. "If these people around here are goin' to be as savage as you say, isn't it our best dodge to get a few miles between us and Crow's Nest—and lay it out in a straight line?"

"We stop and pick up Taxi first," said Christian.

Gregor threw up his hands with a shout of dismay.

"Are you a clean fool? Are you goin' to be a hog, Barry?" he cried. "We've got the coin. We're loaded down with it. Are you goin' to risk everything in order to sink a slug of lead in that wildcat, that Taxi? Can't we leave him for another trip?"

"I've got him marked down. He's waiting, like a horse in a stall," said Christian. "D'you think that ten times this money would be worth to me what it would mean to brush Taxi out of my way for good and all?"

The other stared at him.

"Barry," he said at last, "you *are* crazy. You're blood crazy!" Christian looked back at him with an impassive face.

"Then we'll separate here," he said. "I thought we'd better go on farther before we divided the loot, but we'll make the cut here, and then each of us can go his own way."

They dismounted, accordingly, and in the shelter of a nest of rocks in the center of the gorge they dumped the contents of both sacks on top of the flat of one of them. The treasure overflowed and ran out on the ground. The wind came and whispered through the precious papers.

"All right," said Duff Gregor, feeling that he was entirely in the hands of this terrible partner. "What percentage do I get?"

"Fifty per cent," said Christian.

Gregor stared. He stared until his mouth opened, though not on speech. "It's more'n I expected," he said finally. "You been all the brains."

The words had been wrung from him. He regretted them instantly. But Christian said: "I always get fifty per cent. I never take more. If I do a job all by myself, I never take more than half. The rest goes to charity, to a friend—it's not my luck to take more than half."

The strangeness of that superstition staggered Gregor. It was hard for him to feel gratitude. He felt no gratitude now but merely wonder. Then he found an explanation.

All men, he told himself, who were geniuses, had something twisted and queer in their make-ups. They all had to have something queer. It was what struck the balance. Christian was a genius. There was no doubt that this devil had plenty of excess brains, but he was also a freak. It was better, Gregor felt, to have only normal brains like his own, than to have the excess talent of a Barry Christian and to throw away opportunities.

In a case like this, for instance, he was being overpaid twice, and all because Christian was the silly victim of a superstition!

He did not pause to shake his head over the thing. He started, at once, counting the money.

Even at that business, Christian was three or four times as rapid as his less-gifted companion. And when it came to estimating the value of the negotiable paper that they had taken, Christian seemed able to get at the truth in a glance. They added up the result, and Barry Christian it was who announced:

"We've each got a shade over two hundred thousand dollars, old son. This little job is going to make history. And—here's where we say good-by."

But a wild enthusiasm overmastered the more cautious instinct of Duff Gregor when he heard the size of the fortune that had come into his hands. He shouted:

"No, Barry! I was talking like a fool. I'm goin' to stay with you. We'll clean up Taxi together, and then we'll go and conquer the whole world!"

CHAPTER 13

Taxi's Surprise

Taxi had been awake all night. As the dawn began, he remained hunched over his table in the shack. He was only partially dressed because he had been about to go to bed when his attention had become absorbed in a work of art. He had one shoe on and one off. His coat had been thrown aside. His necktie had been removed and his shirt was open at the throat. One of his cuffs was unbuttoned.

Most men would have caught a severe chill from exposure in such a garb as this while sitting motionless through the cold of the night, and Taxi had hardly stirred a hand for many hours. But he was warmed by the eager, electric vibration of his enthusiasm that cherished the vital spark in him. He had not so much as rolled or lighted a cigarette. He was unaware of any need of the body. His throat was dry, but he did not heed hunger, cold, or thirst.

And the work of art which was before him on the table, and to which he had given his whole soul during the entire night, was a steel lock, not overlarge.

It was, in fact, a very neat and fine bit of metal work; but what interested Taxi was not the goodness of the material but the clever brain of the inventor who had created this master lock. It was guaranteed to baffle all the brains in the criminal world. Nothing but the power to blast it to pieces would be sufficient to open that lock, the maker had declared, and Taxi had specially bought the lock so that he could work on it. It was a habit of his to get the finest productions of the locksmith and then lavish on them his own keen talents. Usually the investment of a mere hour or two was enough to solve the problem, but on this occasion he had been up the entire night working with his various picklocks.

He had taken out his set of burglar's tools which he carried about with him in various parts of his clothes. Tools made as if they were precious jewels, without regard to expense, all constructed of alloys of incredible strength and lightness, tools so slender that they would have crumpled in the grip of an ordinary workman. But though they were so meager that most of them could be unjointed and hidden under the seams of his clothes, yet in the expert fingers of Taxi those little tools could cut their way through the secrets of the most powerful safes.

The principle, with Taxi, was to find the right point, the weak unit in the chain, and then apply brains and a cutting edge. Failure was a thing to which he was a stranger, simply because he would not admit its possibility.

He did not need most of those tools for the delicate task which was in his hands now, but he had laid out a great portion of them here simply because he liked to have them around him. They inspired him with the recollection of many another knotty problem in the past which, he, unaided, had solved.

Consider him now, leaning over that fine lock with half-closed eyes, looking like a poet who, with pen poised above the paper, waits for the voice of the muse. But, instead of a pen, the sensitive fingers of Taxi held a bit of watch-spring steel. His finely made, handsome face showed no expression except, now and then, for a slight flicker of the nostrils.

But in reality he was almost a maniac with nerves. He could have leaped up from his chair and torn at his hair, screaming. Wild horses of desperation and fury were ready to tear him. And the more he controlled himself, the more wildly his nerves raged to have their expression.

He wanted to catch up the lock and dash it against a rock. He wanted to smash it to pieces. He wanted to rush out and set fire to the trees and curse and yell and rave as the flames soared in a terrible wave over the mountainsides.

Instead, he held himself firmly in hand. That little smile that occasionally curled at his lips was the stern sign of his tyranny over his flesh and his weaker spirits. He despised the elements which were working to master him.

The night wore away into the gray of the morning. He was not aware of the change. Born and bred as he had been in the darkness of the great cities of the East, he knew little about sunrises and sunsets. Electric light had shone on nine-tenths of the hours of his life until, at last, something hardly more than chance had brought him west and into sudden and vital contact with Jim Silver.

There in the West he had remained, but always his heart was turning back to the land he knew—that underworld in which he had been a hero. He was a hero in the West, also, with a growing name, because he was the one man in the world whom Jim Silver would willingly take on a trail. He had shown himself fearless, able to endure the most devilish torments rather than be untrue to his friend. And for all of these ample reasons he was admired and respected.

He was so admired and respected that the officers of the law who came west, now and again, on some old trail that pointed in his direction, were never able to get their hands on him. Or, if they did, public opinion, expressed by the heavy public hand, tore him suddenly away from the grasp of the law.

But now, as he sat there in the shack among the Rockies, his mind and his soul were lost in the work of the locksmith, and the only environment of which he was at all aware was that of crime—the one surrounding with which he was truly familiar.

He had even forgotten that it was not an electric or a gas light by which he worked, but only the tremulous, yellow flame of a lamp. He was by no means conscious of the beginnings of the day. The universe had no existence for him. He seemed more and more the perfect type of the dreamer or the abstruse speculator, except, now and again, when he raised his eyes and glanced aside, for then it was that the pale brightness of his eyes showed something worthy to be feared, though those side glances were directed only at the inward processes of his own mind.

Such was the mental state of Taxi when a shadow stirred.

Ordinarily that shadow would not have been seen by usual mortals, simply because other men would not have had the doors of their cabins open at this hour in the day.

Neither would it have been seen by Taxi himself, no matter what the sharpness of his senses, except that he was so deeply involved in his speculations that in this very instant he was drawing close, he felt, to the solution of his problem. Therefore, his subconscious mind was in total charge of him, and the subconscious mind of Taxi, like that of a cat or a wolf, was a very safe guardian, no matter how the master slept.

That subconscious self it was that suddenly jarred the mind of Taxi back to full awareness of the world, just in time to see a mere shadow, a mere hint of a guess at a living form, glide into a patch of shrubbery hardly fifty feet from the door.

It was a shock to Taxi to come out of the world of the mind into the world of fact. It was a shock to him to see, around him, the wretched rawness of the rickety old cabin in which he was sitting, and the huge, grim beauty of the mountains of the morning beyond his door. It was a shock to say to himself, like a guilty creature of the night: "This is the day. What are you doing here where the things of the day will soon be able to see you?"

But it was still the subconscious mind that brought an automatic pistol into his hand. He did not have to think twice. If it were an animal, there would be no great harm in hitting it; if it were a man—what chance in a million of that?—men should not be furtively stealing about a lone cabin at this hour of the day.

And then all the nervous rage which had been boiling in Taxi overflowed. He gritted his teeth so hard that they groaned together, and he sent a burst of three bullets right into the brush.

A curse and a yell answered him, and then a rifle shot that clipped through both walls of the cabin at about the level of his head.

He disregarded the open door and danger beyond it, however. There was also the window and its battered shutter to the side, and he sprang to guard against a flank attack, without even having to hesitate to make sure that this was the right course.

What he saw beyond that window gave pause even to his steel-cold courage, for yonder, in the act of springing to get to shelter behind an outcropping of rocks, was none other than the great Barry Christian, no longer with the make-up of Thomas Bennett, though still in Bennett's clothes.

It was such a crushing blow to the wits of Taxi that he hesitated through a priceless interval—an interval, let us say, of a hundredth part of a second—and the result was that he fired just a foot too late. Barry Christian was already in shelter behind the rocks, and his return fire was drilling through and through the cabin.

Taxi dropped to one knee, gasping.

If Barry Christian was the reality behind the man who had appeared to be Bennett, then who was the Jim Silver that Taxi had met in the hotel at Crow's Nest?

He remembered now—it was not the first time he had thought about it—the husky, faint voice of Silver, the dimness of the room, the strange order which sent him out of town to wait for further instructions. All of these might well be the devices of men trying to keep him from seeing, in a clear light, that it was not Jim Silver in person who had been in that room.

And yet, what man in the world would be such a fool as to attempt to play the role of Jim Silver?

Well, why not? There was nothing so very peculiar about the appearance of Silver. And, after all, his habit of living chiefly in the wilderness had shielded him from the eyes of most men. He was chiefly known, to be sure, by the silver spots in his hair above the temples that had given him his name, and by the magnificence of his horse, Parade.

At any rate, it was certain that yonder was Bennett, that Bennett was Barry Christian, and that, therefore, Christian had been in the hotel room where Taxi thought that he had talked with Silver.

The thing reduced to an absurdity. A devil and an angel would meet for conversation far more easily than Silver and Christian could be confined to one room.

It was not Jim Silver, then, that he had seen. It was the order of a masquerader, a scoundrelly pretender, that had sent Taxi out there into the country to wait until Christian and his friend were ready to take his scalp!

No wonder that the reeling brain of Taxi needed a few moments to absorb these facts.

He was roused to the need for action by the plucking fingers of a bullet that had flicked through the loose flap of shirt that hung at his side.

Barry Christian, with his rifle fire, was methodically raking the floor of the cabin, shooting only a few inches above it. There would be no time to burrow down into the ground and secure safety in this manner, as in a trench. And, in the meantime, the second enemy, the unknown man, the false Silver, was firing either hip-high or breast-high.

Even if Taxi put off the fatal moment for an instant, he could be sure that they would soon have him.

CHAPTER 14

The Posse

Taxi looked about him. He was so desperate that he even considered standing up on the table, so that it might be unlikely that the bullets would strike any part of him except the legs. Then he took note of another possibility.

The cabin was built with a center post, to the top of which were led four beams from the corners of the shack, as though the original builder had planned to build a little attic for a storeroom. Where those four beams met, it was possible that he might find a sort of humble crow's nest in which he could be safe from any but high-ranging bullets.

He stepped onto the table, jumped, caught the rafter nearest to him, and swung up onto the top of it. Lying out across the top of the beams, he was then fairly safe. The trouble was, however, that he could not see the enemy if they made a sudden rush attack on the house.

The rifle fire ended momentarily.

"Taxi! Oh, Taxi!" called the voice of Barry Christian. "Come out and talk to me." Taxi said nothing.

"Taxi," called Christian, "on my word and honor as a gentleman, I won't harm you. Come out here and talk to us. We'll have a truce."

Taxi smiled. He had a very accurate idea of what the word and honor of Barry Christian were worth in such a time as this.

"There's no use holding out on me," said Christian. "I can burn you out, you fool, if you put me to it. But what I really want is a chance to talk with you."

They might, as a matter of fact, burn out Taxi, but in the meantime they would have some trouble. Around the cabin there was nothing but grass, rocks, and brush. If there were a sufficient wind blowing, they might start a pile of dry brush burning and let it roll with the wind against the house. But there was no wind to help them, just now.

Taxi lay still. If he answered, the direction from which his voice came might suggest to the cunning ears of Christian that Taxi was lying well above the level of the floor.

The silence of Taxi brought a few curses from Christian. It was strange how well the voice carried through the stillness of the mountain air.

"Maybe we've nicked him!" called the voice of the second man, from the other side of the cabin. "Maybe he's dead, eh?"

"You can't kill that much poison as cheaply as that," answered Christian.

Taxi smiled a twisted smile at the compliment. He looked down at the table. Half of his soul yearned to be seated there, regardless of flying bullets, at work over the problem of the lock.

Christian was calling: "You let him see you, you wool-headed fool! You let him see you, and I told you that he has eyes like a hawk. I hope he shot a hole through the middle of you."

"He only nicked my cheek," answered the other. "Blast him! I went softer than an owl through the air. How could I guess that he could see me? I thought that he'd be asleep. It was all quiet There was no smoke coming out of the chimney. How could I tell, eh?"

"You could have done what I told you to do," answered Christian. "If I ever tackle a job again with you for a partner—"

He clipped off his speech, and perhaps vented some of his rage by firing three shots in rapid succession through the rotten walls.

Taxi could hear the dull, chugging sounds as the bullets chopped through the rotten timber. He could see the little eyelets of light appear.

The man from the other side had opened in turn, firing sometimes high and sometimes low. They were honeycombing the shack, and it was only a question of time before they whipped some lead into the body of Taxi.

He stood up on the top of the center post. In this manner he could look out of the little triangular window which had been cut in the roof of the shanty, and he saw clearly the jerking muzzle of a rifle as it was fired again and again from the patch of brush. There was no sign of the enemy, but Taxi saw that something had to be risked, even if his position were revealed. He took aim at a point above the rifle and a yard behind it. Then he fired three shots in a row. It was his way, because he liked to group the bullets of an automatic, making them fly like a little spray of water.

He got for a reward a yelp of pain and fear. The rifle disappeared. There was a sound of crashing in the brush.

"Up high!" yelled the voice of Christian's friend. "Up high. He's up near the top of the roof."

"Did he get you?" asked Christian.

"He scraped my shoulder for me. I'm goin' to boil him in oil before I'm finished with him!"

Immediately, the fire centered high on the walls, and Taxi heard the intimate humming of the bullets about his head and body. Another bullet clipped his clothes, drilling through the flap of his trousers leg. He dropped flat to the floor.

It seemed that Christian must have heard the noise, nevertheless, for now a bullet from his side of the house struck the earth and threw a stinging shower of it into the face of Taxi.

He leaped to a far corner of the shack. The eyes of the devil seemed to be following him, looking through the solid wood with ease, for another bullet instantly clipped a lock of hair from his head. It was the end. They had him on the run, and they would beat the life out of him with the flying lead in a few moments, he knew.

And then the voice of Christian's companion loudly yelped: "They're comin'! They're right in the pass, now. Get out of here, Barry!"

A terrible oath ripped out of the throat of Christian. He fired six shots, high and low, in rapid succession. Perhaps he was emptying his rifle. Then there was silence.

Taxi counted to twenty before he ventured to the door of the shack. It was not a sham to draw him outside, for now he could hear the distant muttering of the hoofs of many horses, and immediately afterward there was the galloping beat of a pair receding from the neighborhood of the cabin.

There was no use mounting his own horse to pursue Barry Christian and one other through mountains that Barry knew like a book. And, therefore, Taxi sat down at the lock and began to work over it with the bit of watch-spring steel!

He was lost in the problem. He was still very deep in it when the noise of the horses increased to a thundering that shook the earth and made the stove jingle softly in the corner of the shack. With the tenth part of his mind, Taxi was aware of these things. The rest of his wits were entirely concentrated on the problem of the lock, when the squeaking of saddle leather announced that men were dismounting near the cabin.

Then they came pouring in.

He gave another twist to the picklock. It would not work— yes, something was yielding.

"It's Taxi," said a loud voice. "It's his side kicker, Taxi."

Another said: "Taxi, what—"

"Shut up," said Taxi. And suddenly the lock had yielded to his hands. He pulled it open. It lay mastered before him. In ten seconds, on the next try, he would know how to master that delicate combination. After all, it had been simple—but unexpected—the way all good brain work is apt to be.

At last he looked up as a big fellow in a checkered flannel shirt came up to him, smelling strongly of horse sweat, and dropped a hand on his shoulder. "We want some talk out of you!" said the stranger.

Taxi raised his pale, overbright eyes and stared into the other's face. "Take your hand off my shoulder!" he commanded.

The hand was instantly taken away as one of the other men said: "Look out, Mack! He's poison."

Mack stood back a little, but he spread his legs as though bracing himself to endure a shock.

"I'll take my hand off you, but maybe not for long. Your dirty skunk of a partner, Jim Silver, has been up here, and we want—"

He dodged, but too late. Taxi, coming out of his chair like a cat, lodged the bony ridge of his knuckles on the point of Mack's jaw and dropped him staggering back into the arms of some of his friends.

Then, for a split part of a second, Taxi expected death to spout from the muzzles of a dozen leveled guns. Yet not a shot was fired, for another man said: "Mack's been rushin' things too fast. Wait a minute. Here, you, Taxi. Open up and talk. You talk, or we *will* raise hell with you. You know that Silver's been play actin' watchman down at Henry Wilbur's bank in Crow's Nest. Now he's robbed the bank and gone—he and his side kicker. They've been up here to see you. Likely they've left some of the loot with you. If they have, we're goin' to get it. And we wanta know where they told you they were headin'."

CHAPTER 15

Silver's Arrival

There are times when words won't serve. Taxi felt that one of these times had come. He never liked the weight of many eyes on him. There was a guilty something in him that made him prefer dark loneliness to the public gaze. The same instinct, from a different and a guiltless cause, worked in Jim Silver, and that had helped to make the two men friends. They knew how to spend a silent day and night together without thinking hostile thoughts of one another.

Taxi could only say the first and the greatest truth, about this matter, that sprang into his head, which was simply: "Jim Silver would never take a job as the watchman of a bank." Someone laughed loudly.

"Sure he didn't. But he took a job as the robber! He walked right in there and made fools of us, and he walked off again with the coin. He's been up here. He's seen you, Taxi, and he's told you about his plans. There ain't any doubt about it."

"There's a doubt that it was Jim Silver," said Taxi.

"What?" came the shout. "Doubt, d'you say? Even down to the silver spots over his temples and the gold and shine of Parade, it was Jim Silver, all right!"

Taxi considered.

"We're losin' time," said Mack, rubbing his swollen jaw and staring hungrily at Taxi. "I vote that we count to ten, and then, if he don' t speak, see if we can drag some talk out of him at the end of a lariat!"

"You can't drag nothin' out of him," doubted another speaker. "Not if Jim Silver is in the case. You can't drag nothin' out. Not even Barry Christian was able to do that, and Barry had time to work on him, they say!"

"Are we goin' to stand around here and let a little crook out of the East gum up the deal for us?" shouted Mack.

"I say it wasn't Silver," said Taxi quietly. "Silver's my friend. Would he do work like this?"

He pointed at the walls of the shack, through which eyeholes had been recently drilled by bits cleaner than ever an auger bored.

"What does that prove?" Mack said. "Taxi just stepped outside, and they drilled a few holes through the house to prove that they wasn't his friends. But it's all a lie, and you'll find that the whole bunch of loot has been cached here with Taxi. Don't that make a plan for you? The pair of 'em do the dirty work down there in Crow's Nest, and Taxi waits up here to take the loot! What's simpler than that?"

"Would he be fool enough to start a cannonade that was sure to lead the lot of you right up on his trail?" asked Taxi.

This gave even Mack pause, but only for an instant.

"He knew that we was comin' right up the pass after him, anyways. It didn't take much time. One of 'em did the shootin' while you and the other one hid the loot. Taxi, walk us to that stuff."

"I'll tell you one reason why you're wrong," said Taxi. He pointed to the hole that had been shot in his shirt. The skin had been barely pricked, enough to let out a red stain of blood.

There was a sudden grunt of interest, a sound such as a man makes when a blow lands on him solidly.

Taxi leaned down and pointed to the flap of his trousers. There was another hole bitten through the cloth, there.

One by one, the men crowded nearer. There were thirty of them filling up all the available space. Gloomy conviction appeared in their faces, though Mack now cried out: "All part of the fake! They shoot a coupla holes in the clothes of Taxi—"

"Close enough to cut his skin, eh?" said one of the men. "Don't be a fool, Mack! Boys, we gotta ride! Whatever Taxi is, he ain't in on this deal. If Jim Silver is mean enough to turn crooked, he's mean enough to double-cross a friend of his like Taxi, too."

"You talk like a half-wit," said the calm, gentle voice of Taxi. "Tell me this—would Jim Silver and Barry Christian be riding together?"

"Who said they were? It's Silver and Tom Bennett," answered a posse man.

"Bennett is Barry Christian," said Taxi, "and your Jim Silver is some crook made up to look like my friend."

Incredulous heads were shaken. Only in one or two pairs of eyes appeared the least flicker of doubt.

"There's nothing here," urged a number of the men. "Let's get out and start moving. Silver's gaining ground on us at every jump!"

"Let him get a lead. Who could catch Parade, anyway?" asked another.

"That's true," said another. "But we gotta keep travelin'. They ain't *both* got a Parade under 'em."

They streamed out of the shack, and Mack, still scowling at Taxi, called out as he mounted his horse:

"Keep out of my path, brother. And, if you've got much sense, you won't bother around the town of Crow's Nest, neither. Jim Silver is wanted there, right now, but his friends ain't!" That was the last warning, as the cavalcade poured back through the trees to take the main road across the pass.

It was not the direction which Christian and his companion had taken, but Taxi did not try to correct the men, for he knew that his advice was wanted no more than he had wanted the advice of Mack.

One thing was perfectly clear to him, and this was that he must ride at once for the town of Crow's Nest. If the false Jim Silver had done harm there, if the crime had actually been the robbing of the famous bank, then it was high time for the friends of the real Jim Silver to appear on the scene to discover what had actually happened.

It was at about this time that the true Jim Silver sent Parade up the last slope toward the town of Crow's Nest. It had been a hard ride from the forest of yellow birches, where the bearded man with the bright eyes had given him the information that made him speed toward the town. He had made a quick trip. Parade had traveled as only Parade knew how to move over rough and smooth, and yet, for all his speed, Jim Silver was arriving late by a few vital hours.

He was very weary, but weariness was a thing to which he was accustomed, and which he knew how to master so as to leave his mind fresh and his body prepared for hard action. Out of the power of his will he could refresh himself sufficiently.

He was not received, now, as his alias had been welcomed not many days before. He was well into the town, in fact, before he was sighted. And then it was the solitary, shrill voice of a woman that sent the news pealing down the main street of Crow's Nest:

"Jim Silver's come back! Jim Silver's come back!"

After that, men began to appear. There was no cheering. Every man who appeared had a gun in his hand, a sight so strange that Silver could hardly believe his eyes. No one called out to him. There was no waving of hands.

The heart of Jim Silver was so free from vanity that he felt no real pain at this lack of a reception, but he was puzzled by the grimness of the faces that stared at him.

If the grown-ups were so silent, at least the little boys and girls should have been running out, clapping their hands and yelling with pleasure at the sight of the great Parade. But, instead of giving him the slightest greeting, the children remained in the background, agape, silent, and mothers could be seen gathering in their offspring as though there had been danger of an approaching storm.

As Silver rode on, he was aware that men were swarming out into the street behind him.

Others had gathered ahead of him, along the sidewalks, and still he made out that every man of the lot was heavily armed!

It was stranger than a dream. If he had ridden into a bandit city where every man was wanted by the law, he might have expected some such greeting as this, but he could not be prepared for it among the law-abiding.

Then, as though at a signal given, the men ahead of him poured out into the street and entirely blocked his way.

Parade stopped, unbidden, and lifted his magnificent head. Silver, without glancing back, felt the pressing forward of the crowd at his rear. There were at least three hundred men, all armed, now ahead of him or behind him. The silence was deadly. Other men were coming in the distance, on the run. And now, as he sat in the saddle, he found the crowd edging closer, becoming more compact. He would have been worse than a blind man if he had not known that they meant trouble for him.

"Well, boys, what's in the air?" he said calmly.

There was no response to this, for an instant. Then an old, leaning fellow with a trapper's fur cap on his head, and a double-barreled shotgun in his hands, stepped out a little in advance of his fellows and said, in a drawling voice:

"Jim, I dunno what to make of you. I always been told that you was right bright. You was bright enough to pull the wool over the eyes of everybody for a long spell. But d'you really think that we're such doggone fools that we'd let you come back to town now and bluff us out after you been and robbed the bank?"

And another voice, far back in the crowd, yelled out suddenly: "Silver, ain't you been seen ridin' out of Crow's Nest with your partner, Bennett?"

Silver looked them over with a grim thrill of understanding. All was reasonably clear to him now. These people had all been robbed! And the blame was thrown on him! Whoever it was that had worn his name must have been made up marvelously well in his likeness. He had come down here to prevent a great fraud from being practiced. It seemed that he had only arrived in time to be punished for the crime of another man.

He was not frightened, simply because fear did not know the way into his great heart, but he was shocked and awed by a thing that he had never encountered before in all the days of his life—the seasoned and grim hatred of law-abiding men.

He had heard it said, more than once, that no crowd of thugs is ever half so unreasoning, so ferocious, as a throng of the honest citizens, because the mere consciousness of honesty is apt to make the members of the crowd feel that every emotion in the heart is justifiable and should be followed with safety. These fellows before him had seemed at first merely antagonistic. Now he saw that they meant murder or its equivalent.

"Friends," he said, "this is a cheat that has been worked on you. Some man has been here in my name, but I swear that this is the first time that either I or Parade have been on the streets of your town. I've never been in Crow's Nest before!"

A loud yell of incredulity and rage answered him.

"Partner," said the old trapper, "can I believe that you're goin' to try to tell us that the Jim Silver who was here before was just a kind of a shadder of you? That he was made up like a play actor to look like you? Is that what I gotta listen to? Jim, I'm an old man to listen to that—and when you robbed that bank so doggone clean, you took fifteen hundred dollars of money that it cost me twenty years to save! That was the money to bury me, and now I'm goin' to have it back from you, or else I'm goin' to have that much of your hide!"

This was a long speech, but perhaps it was needed for the sake of rousing the crowd to a fever heat. The anger and the desire to act had been there before in every heart. There was hardly a man in the lot that had not been robbed in the looting of the bank. These were men accustomed to the face of action and ready for it now.

Still the tremendous reputation of this man overawed and held them back with the recollection of the thousands of deeds of heroism with which he had ennobled his own name and the whole West. They could not lift a hand against the greatness of his fame, no matter how much their pocketbooks had suffered.

Then came the speech of the old trapper who, starting calmly, had built up to a shouting climax in which he shook his shotgun at the head of Silver.

One man cried: "But that don't look to me like the gent that's been around town here claiming to be Jim Silver!"

There was a yell of rage at the mere suggestion. Two or three of the crowd—neighbors of that unfortunate speaker—picked him up and hoisted him on their shoulders. "Here's a fool that says it ain't the same as the other Jim Silver!" called one.

"Boys!" screamed the unlucky fellow. "I swear that don't look to me the same as the other chestnut, either. It's bigger and more to it, and—"

He was dropped to his feet, a hard fist knocked him flat, and the crowd trampled over his body as it pressed in on Jim Silver.

If they would do that much to a man who merely dared to lift his voice in defense of what honest eyes saw, what would they do to a man against whom they really had a murderous grudge? Jim Silver saw the workings of their fingers, and it seemed to him that his flesh was already under their hands. It seemed to him that he was already being torn.

CHAPTER 16

Wilbur's Declaration

There was another man in that town who had been torn, though not by physical hands, a little earlier in the morning. That was Henry Wilbur, who sat, not in his ransacked bank, where the work of his life had been swept away, but in his house.

He had gone down to the bank and had written in chalk with his own hand across the front door:

I shall sell all my personal property and apply the proceeds to the payment of the losses incurred by the robbery of this bank. Every depositor shall receive something on every dollar of his deposits.

(Signed) HENRY WILBUR

Even that gallant declaration had not brought a single cheer from the crowd which watched him. They looked on him, rather, with hostile eyes. They began to remember ugly tales that they had heard about bankers in other days. Perhaps men are fools if they intrust their money to banks, they thought, and a hole in the ground would be a better place.

With mute hostility, then, they had stared after poor Wilbur as he walked with a high head through the crowd and climbed the hill to his house. He kept a bright face. He was trying to strip away from his mind the dreadful sense of loss. He was trying to say to himself that every blow may be endured.

When he went into the house, he was met by his wife and daughter. He took the hands of his wife and said to her:

"Molly, it's true. I'm sorry to tell you that every penny has been cleaned out of the bank safe. There's not a nickel left except a few bonds that are not negotiable. Not enough to count. Not enough to make a penny on the dollar."

Mrs. Wilbur was as small, as withered, as dry, as her husband was large and robust. She made a gesture with one lean, bloodless hand, as though to put away the facts that had just been spoken, and, peering into the face of her husband, she asked:

"Henry, you're not making up your mind to do any foolish thing, are you?" He patted her shoulder and smiled down at her.

"That depends on what you call foolish," he said.

She stood back from him, as though she wanted a little distance to see more clearly both his face and the dreadful thought that had come into her mind. For she knew him very well indeed, and all the workings of that brave and gentle heart of his. Her voice came out chokingly:

"Henry, you've lost more than anyone else. You're not going to throw away your personal holdings to pay a part of the losses?"

Then, without waiting for the answer, she demanded: "How much was taken away?"

He looked at his daughter, and she nodded. She was pale, but steady as a rock. He had always guessed and hoped that she was chiefly his child. Now he knew it.

She said: "Mother, we'd better not trouble Father now. There's nothing to do except the right thing, and he knows better what that is than we do."

"I want to know!" exclaimed the wife. "Henry Wilbur, how much was taken from the bank vault?"

He hesitated, and then he said:

"Over—four—hundred—thousand—dollars."

As he spoke, the weight of the words inclined his head a little. A wild screech came out of the throat of his wife.

"Henry, Henry!" she screamed at him. "You're not going to throw away everything to pay a part of that? You're not going to—"

"Mother!" said the girl. "We have to leave him alone. We have to. There's only one thing to do, and he knows what that should be."

Mrs. Wilbur's head dropped on her shoulder. She was almost fainting, and between them, her husband and her daughter got her stretched on her bed. There Ruth Wilbur worked over her until she had recovered enough to break into wild sobbing.

"He'll give it all away!" mourned Mrs. Wilbur. "We'll die in paupers' graves. Oh, what have we done to deserve it? What have we done to deserve this? Ruth, child, darling, he loves you more than the rest of the world. Go and fall on your knees. Beg him not to ruin us. Remind him that he owes something to your future. He'll turn us out on the streets. He'll sell the house from over our heads. Go to him! Go to him!"

The girl went—not to fall on her knees and beg, however.

She found him in the library, dictating to his stenographer. He was, in fact, drawing up a list of his personal assets. As for his properties in mines and timbers, he knew that well enough. The more personal items, however, required thought, and he was giving his attention to them as the girl entered, softly, unobserved.

Harry Craig, Wilbur's secretary, was drawing up the list as his chief dictated. It was typical of Henry Wilbur that he should have chosen a man like Craig to be his secretary, loading him with favors, nursing his investments, making him wealthy enough to be independent.

Harry Craig had been born into the world with a twisted body and a half-paralyzed left side. He was so ugly that people could not endure his presence, and, therefore, his mind became as twisted as his body, until Henry Wilbur, out of great pity in his heart, took Craig in hand and gradually untwisted the tangles of his dark and bitter soul. To Craig, Wilbur was more than a man. He was a religion. For Craig, there was Henry Wilbur, and behind him, far away, unimportant, there was the rest of the world.

Now he sat crookedly in his chair, resting his deformed, gloved left hand on the edge of the paper on which he was writing. He peered aslant at what he wrote and seemed to take no interest in anything except the beauty of the letters which he was forming.

As for Henry Wilbur, he kept his head up and his eye calm, but his heart was dying in him, and his daughter knew it. She knew everything about him. She always had, from the time she was a small thing. She stood there by the door, silent, unobserved, and watched her father in his torment. Tears began to run down her face, not because she was sad about him, but because she felt he was so glorious.

He was saying: "That brings us to the bank building and the ground it stands on. It has some value. It's in a good position, and when a new bank is set up in Crow's Nest, probably the new concern won' t be able to do better than take over the old building. We can put down the value as twenty-five thousand dollars, I think. Next, there's this house and the land on which it stands."

"This house?" said Craig, without looking up. "Yes, this house," answered Wilbur.

"Your home?" asked Craig, jerking his head so that he could peer into the face of the banker.

"Yes, my home. It has to go. Everything has to go," said Wilbur.

The girl took in her breath slowly. She had guessed it; her mother, even, had guessed it. Everything was to go in order to redeem the losses which had fallen upon the depositors of the town. The tears stopped running down her face, because she was supremely glad that there was one such man in the world. Her color changed. Her eyes brightened. She began to shine with beauty of the sort that time cannot corrupt in the eyes nor rub out of the face.

"The house," said Wilbur, "ought to bring in about fifteen thousand dollars. It cost a good deal more than that to build, but this blow is apt to flatten things out in Crow's Nest, for the time being. Prices will be low. Say another five thousand for the land we've built on. That makes twenty thousand. Then there are the furnishings."

"The furniture, Mr. Wilbur?" said Craig.

"Yes," said Wilbur. "Furniture doesn't bring in much, but some of the rugs have a more or less stable value. Then there are the books."

Wilbur ran his eyes over the lines of books which filled the wall spaces in the room. His happy times of rest had been spent in that room. It was the Mecca of his life to which he retired to be with his higher self. Books had always been his care and affection. He could name every book on these shelves by its size and position. He knew this room as he knew the palm of his hand.

"Altogether, furniture and books and all, put down ten thousand dollars. I hope we'll be able to get more, but in forced sales, one never knows. Now what does that bring the total to?"

"There are some other things that could be added," said Craig, in a hard, rasping voice. "Such as what?" asked Wilbur.

"Your wife's jewelry. And your daughter's."

"My wife—may be persuaded," said Wilbur, "but for the time being it will be best not to list her personal possessions. Of course, whatever Ruth has will be sold along with my own things."

He spoke with perfect confidence, and suddenly, as she listened, she felt that she was rewarded and repaid beforehand for any pain that life could give her in all the years to come. She had his utter faith, and nothing else was of importance.

As her father spoke her name, he turned his head suddenly, and saw her. The sight of her got him quickly out of his chair. Craig turned about and made an odd, gurgling sound in the hollow of his throat.

"I'm sorry, my dear," said Henry Wilbur. "Everything has to go. Your things and my things. It would mean a continual shame to me if every effort were not made to pay—"

He had begun to come toward her with a rather fumbling, uncertain step. She met him before he could go far, and measured him with her outstretched hands just the right distance so that she could look squarely into his eyes.

"If you did anything else," she said, "I'd be ashamed of you. If you weren't going to throw everything away for the sake of your good name, I'd be ashamed."

He had been very flushed as he approached her; now he grew pale with a sudden access of emotion of another sort.

"Do you hear, Craig?" he said. "Do you hear? One person understands and—and—"

He made a vague, pawing gesture with one hand, bent to the side, and then sprawled on the floor.

Ruth dropped on her knees, grabbed his vest, and ripped it open. The buttons came crackling off. She put her ear over his heart. He was fat. There was a muffling layer of flesh between his heart and her ear. She could hear nothing—he was dead! No, then she got it, a subdued, hesitant fluttering, guessed at rather than known.

Craig threw himself at his master. He grabbed at the girl with his sound hand and with his useless, gloved claw.

"You've killed him!" he screamed at her. "You've murdered him! Get away from him!" Ruth jumped up, saying:

"Open the window. Throw water on him. Fan his face. I'm getting the doctor!" She was already running for the door as she spoke the last words.

CHAPTER 17

A Woman's Power

In the next room she saw her mother. Mrs. Wilbur had got up from her bed when she heard the scream of Craig. Now, with her false hair spilling in one direction and her real hair falling in another, with her dress loosened at the throat and her eyes staring, she came tottering toward her daughter, holding out her hands. And she looked to Ruth Wilbur like the living picture of the ruined fortunes of the house.

"What's happened, Ruth?" she cried.

The girl tried to dodge. One wonderfully strong hand caught her and attached itself to her. She twisted about silently and struck the hand away. Then she ran on from the house and down the steps.

From the main street came an uproar of voices. A thousand people seemed to be shouting one phrase, but they were out of rhythm with one another, and, therefore, it was simply a great obscurity of formless sound that she heard.

She was on the back of a mustang which was tethered at the hitch rack in front of the house. There was always a horse ready there, day and night. It was a rule that her father had made, and perhaps it would be the saving of his life, now.

She sent that mustang hurtling down the long slope of the driveway toward the street. She had time to remember that she was not wearing a divided skirt and, therefore, her appearance was not modest; it was such that her mother would almost prefer death to such an exhibition. She was able to think of that, and smile vaguely at it.

Then the mustang began to pitch. It was full of kinks, and she laid the quirt into the mean little beast savagely. In half a dozen strokes it felt the pain of the whiplash more than the ugliness of its own temper, and it had straightened out to a dead run as the girl shot out through the gateway into the street.

The air was filled with a filmy cloud of dust that thickened, two blocks away, into a heavy white mist. There were hundreds of people in the street, packing in closer and closer, like iron filings over a magnet. And the center of attraction was a tall man on a great chestnut horse. She knew it was a stallion by the forelock and the arch of the neck like the bending of a mighty bow.

Hands were being raised against the rider by men farther back in the crowd. Those in front were threatening, also. They were about to drag that man from his horse and kill him, and she knew it. But that didn't matter. What *did* matter was that the doctor's house was straight down this street, and there was no other way of getting to it. Not unless she turned back and rode clear around the bridge that arched across the gulch and so, by tortuous way, up to the doctor's house from the other side.

However, there was no time for that. Her father lay dying on the carpet of the library. Perhaps he was dead already. She had to get through that crowd. If they had to kill that man—well, she hoped they would kill him now so that she could ride through as they scattered.

She would try the outskirts, and try to press through across the sidewalk.

She turned in. The frightened mustang began to pitch and squeal with fear. It helped to clear a path before them with its antics. Men cursed and dodged out of the way.

She saw that she was going to win through, and the instant that she was sure of that, her mind cleared so that she was able to hear the words that the crowd shouted. Every man had a different phrase of hatred and contempt, but all of them were shouting about Jim Silver. They were saying that they would show him that he could not bluff the entire town of Crow's Nest. They would show him the justice of the greatest jurist in the world—Judge Lynch. One man was waving a rope over his head, yelling that he had the hemp that would break the neck of crooked Jim Silver.

It was Jim Silver. That was the chestnut stallion, and there was the man who had robbed her father's bank—the man whose indirect hand had stretched Henry Wilbur on the floor, perhaps dying.

She hoped they would tear Jim Silver to pieces! There was no feminine mercy or pity, no tenderness or horror in her. Her body was as tough and strong as the body of a boy. She had done her share of hunting big game, too, and her mind was as grim and stern as the mind of a man when she was roused.

She was roused now, and, staring across the heads of the crowd, through the mist of the dust, she hated the rider with all her heart. It was as she stared that the sudden realization came to her that this was not the face of the man who had leaned above her in her father's garden and taken her in his arms and kissed her. There was no beast in this man. He was calmly waiting at the hands of that crowd for the thing that could not be avoided. That other fellow would not have been able to endure. He would have had his guns out, by this time, shooting, killing before he was killed. Or else he would be screeching out appeals. But this man was simply waiting.

She looked again and was sure. There was a resemblance between that other Jim Silver and this one. A mere resemblance, and that was all. But the crowd was seeing what it wanted to see. It wanted to have the bank robber in its hands and it was determined that this was the man.

Ruth cried out: "It's not the man you want! You're wrong! He's not the man!"

But her voice was piping and thin in her own ears, against the growing roar of the crowd. For the tumult was gathering head and rising in crescendo. Action would follow very quickly.

She looked wildly about her. A gap had opened. She could break through and get to the doctor and bring him back on the run to her father's house. But still she could not leave this place until she had struck one blow for that big, brown-faced fellow who was so calmly waiting for death.

It was the real Jim Silver. She knew that. Truth, when it strikes the heart, rings it like a bell. It was the real Parade on which he sat. There was something more beautiful, more massive, more wildly free about the head of the famous horse. This was the real hero, and the robber was a pretender.

Then she saw the sheriff.

Sheriff Dick Williams was doing his best to break into the crowd. He was taking men by the shoulders and trying to draw them back. He could not succeed. Only now and again he pried two men apart and pressed between them, yelling that he represented the law, that he must make that rider his prisoner. Fists were suddenly raised, but no man dared to strike the representative of the law. The hands remained poised an instant until he was recognized, and then they dropped down again. But he could not make real headway through the mass of the throng. He would only spur them on more quickly to the murder.

The hat of Dick Williams flew off. Ruth Wilbur jammed the mustang straight at his gray, tousled head.

Men turned and yelled savagely at her. She pressed straight ahead. She got the frothing muzzle of the horse at the shoulder of Williams. She leaned forward and screamed at his ear:

"Get up here! We'll ride through!"

He turned a bewildered face toward her.

"That isn't the bank robber! That's not the man who worked in the bank!" she screeched. The sheriff shouted an astonished rejoinder. She could not make out the words in the increasing roar of the many voices. For the time for action had come at last, and the men around Silver were reaching up their hands, grabbing at him.

Dick Williams swung up in the stirrup which she abandoned to him. "Get out of the saddle! Let me ride through!" he shouted in her ear.

"You need a woman. A man can't do anything!" she answered, and she drove the spurs remorselessly deep into the flanks of her horse.

The mustang plunged ahead. Its shoulders hurled the press aside. A man went down, crying out in terror. It seemed to the girl that the horse trampled straight over the fallen body. She spurred again and again. She worked the rowels into the sides of the mustang. It reared and struck out. From those iron-shod hoofs, men shrank away. They yelled curses at her. Hands grabbed at her to pluck her from the saddle. She felt her dress ripping, here and there. The man who was swinging the rope aimed the noose at her. She ducked. The rope knocked her hair out of its coil and sent it down in a bright flood.

But now she was in the midst of the dust cloud and the shouting and close to Jim Silver. It was like being in the middle of a stampede. They were not humans. They were animals, packed close together and hot for murder. She cut at them with her quirt. They twitched their faces around—blind, distorted faces—and saw the man of the law and the desperate girl. They gave back.

She was perfectly right. No man could have done such a thing with that crowd, but a woman was different. There is a certain point west of the Mississippi where a woman becomes different, where something sacred begins to attach to femininity, and that swirling knot of men parted and fell back from Silver, as the girl came up.

She stood up in the stirrups and shouted:

"This isn't the man! This isn't the man who robbed the bank! This isn't the man!"

They couldn't hear her. The men in front were pausing for the instant. Those behind were driving forward, yelling like thunder. Words would mean nothing to them. Ruth pressed her mustang beside the towering stallion. She threw her arm around Jim Silver and still, with her quirt, slashed at the men who were too close.

The sheriff climbed into the saddle behind Silver. He snapped a pair of handcuffs over the wrists of an unresisting prisoner. Then he forced the hands into the air so that the steel could be seen holding the hands of Jim Silver.

That might make some difference to the crowd.

But they forged ahead; no one understood. It seemed to that crowd that a woman had come to her lover in his time of danger, and the edge of their murder lust was turned and blunted. Besides, there was the man of the law, and his steel cuffs were on the robber, as they thought. They fell back from the angry leaping of the quirt. They opened a channel through which the sheriff and the girl and Jim Silver passed.

They pressed across the street, turned a corner where only a scattering of excited men stood in the way, and then stopped in front of a low, squat building—the jail. The door of it opened. They sprang down from their horses. And that was how Jim Silver managed to reach shelter from the mob.

The girl saw the big, swinging shoulders pass through the doorway into interior darkness. She saw the door close again; then she turned the mustang and rode hard to get the doctor.

CHAPTER 18

A Gathering Storm

Henry Wilbur was still stretched on the library carpet when Ruth got the doctor to the house. They had wound a cold towel around his head, put a pillow under his shoulders, and another under his feet. His eyes and his mouth were slightly open. He looked like a dead man, but now and then he could be heard to draw a breath. The breathing had a bubbling sound and seemed, every minute, about to stop.

With the doctor there, they got Wilbur into bed. He lay in a semi-coma. The doctor said that he might lie that way for twenty-four hours and after that—well, no one could tell. The heart was weak—very weak—but it was not a stroke of paralysis. Overload this human soul and the fine steel of it may snap; that was all the doctor could say.

The girl sat for hours and hours at the side of her father. Now and then he would say: "Sell everything." Then she would press his hand and answer: "Everything's all right." She tried to think of something else to say, but that phrase was all that she could use, and every time he heard it, the gathering cloud would pass out of the forehead of the sick man. His breathing became steadier. Late in the afternoon his eyes suddenly opened wide, and he knew what was happening around him.

"Has everything been sold?" he asked. "Everything is going to be sold," she told him.

He considered the ceiling, and remarked: "I seem to have crashed."

"No one could help crashing," she assured him. "Nobody could blame you for crashing. Don't you understand that?"

"All right," he said, "but listen to me. You're my witness. If I pass out—which I'm not going to do—but if I pass out, I want everything sold to help pay back the investors. Listen to me—if everything is sold, I can pay them eighty-five cents on the dollar. Don't let your mother talk you out of the truth. Eighty-five cents on the dollar. I made that money and I also made a good name. A good name is a lot better than money. I want to spend the money to save the name. I'm selfish. You and your mother may starve—but your name will be clean. I don't have to tell you this because you already know it! This is my last will and testament. Now, try to get the lawyer, and I'll get that will into writing."

She got the lawyer. Then she went in and sat beside her mother for a time. The little gray-haired woman lay in a darkened room, moaning softly, and weeping continually.

"It's ruin!" she kept saying, over and over. "It's ruin, ruin, ruin! He's going to turn us out into the street. I'll fight. It's not legal. He's not in his right mind! Oh, Ruth, my poor darling!" The girl went back into the library, and sat there alone, trying to think.

Craig came hobbling in, bringing a letter.

He said, as he gave it to her: "I lost my head when your father fainted. I said some things to you. I'm sorry about that."

"Don't be sorry," said the girl. "I like you better, because you said those things."

Craig shook his head. He hesitated, trying to get out the words that stuck in his throat. "You're the only one that matters to him," he said sharply, and turned about and went hastily out of the room.

It was a very strange thing, she thought, that she should be able to pity Craig, that she should be able to spare that much thought to anyone other than her father, and to the real Jim Silver, who was safely lodged in the jail.

She opened the letter, and it was from Silver. It ran:

Dear Miss Wilbur:

No one can tell how things will turn out. In any case, I want you to have a few words from me before the finish, whatever it may be. I want to tell you, above all, that you did what nobody else in the world could have done.

The sheriff tells me that you were on your way to get the doctor for your father, who was close to death. But that hardly makes what you did for me any more wonderful.

I've never known a man who was the pure steel all the way to the heart, but I can say, now, that I've known one such woman.

They were going to kill me with their bare hands. They were going to smash me up. It would have started in a few seconds. Nothing but a woman could have stopped them. And no woman but you would even have tried.

I have to keep remembering that I'm a stranger to you. It was perfect before, but that makes it more perfect.

Yours,

Jim Silver

She began to smile at the letter, the swiftly running, small writing. One thing in the letter was untrue entirely. They were not strangers.

She went out and found Craig.

"I want to talk to you about Jim Silver," she said. "Why is he still in the jail?"

"Because he can't get out," said Craig.

"Can't get out? Why not?"

Craig began to breathe hard. "You want him free?" he asked. "Of course I do," said the girl.

"The scoundrel that ruined your father?" shouted Craig. "You want him free?"

"Hush," said the girl. "Father will hear you."

"I hope he does!" said Craig. "I hope he finds out, before he dies, that his girl loves a bank robber more than she loves her father! I hope that he finds out the truth about you!"

"Do you really think the man in jail is the robber?" she asked.

"Are there two Jim Silvers in this world? Are you completely out of your head, Ruth?"

"Do you know," said the girl, "that the man the mob was trying to kill was not the man who was working for my father?"

"What?" said Craig.

"I've seen him. I know."

"I heard some sort of nonsense to that effect," said Craig. "The whole town knows that there's a plot on foot to bamboozle the authorities and get the robber out of the hands of justice. But that plot is going to be baffled, even if some wise young women like Ruth Wilbur have been convinced. The townspeople have not been convinced, and the sheriff has not been convinced, either. You can be sure of that because I've seen and talked with him."

"You mean that Dick Williams really thinks that he has the right man there in jail?" she demanded.

"Ruth, Ruth," said the cripple, easily exasperated, "anyone but a woman, and a silly woman at that, would realize that *of course* we have the right man down there in the jail. And the sheriff will keep him there. At least Williams will manage to keep him there until the mob tears down the building and takes the rascal away."

"Do you think that the mob *will* attack the jail?" she asked.

"Will they? I don't know. They ought to, certainly. They've heard something about this same nonsense that has reached your ears, and they are not going to be put off by a ridiculous story of double identity. The people in this town are pretty much worked up, young lady. They know, now, that your father intends to give up his fortune to pay most of the losses of the robbery. They know, besides, that your father is at the point of death, and that's why they want Jim Silver—not for robbery only, but for murder. And they're right."

He was just finishing this tirade when word was brought to the girl that a man wanted to see her.

"Go back to your father," said the bitter cripple. "I'll go and see the man, whoever he is. It's probably another one of the rascals who've been talking nonsense to you."

He went hobbling away to the front door where, outside the screen, he saw a dapper youth in his early twenties, wearing a very neat blue suit with a white flower in his buttonhole. He had on a pair of good chamois gloves that folded down over the backs of his hands, and he was resting one of these hands on a very slender and supple walking stick. He seemed to have walked over the street on winged feet, for there was not a sign of dust on his well-polished shoes. His gray felt hat was tucked jauntily under his arm; and what offended the savage little cripple more than all else was the flawless part and the glossy sleekness of the black hair of this man, who said:

"I believe this is the house of Henry Wilbur, the banker?"

"Do you?" said Craig, openly snarling.

"In that case," said the stranger, "will you be good enough to ask Miss Wilbur if I may have the pleasure of speaking with her for a few minutes?"

"I will *not* be good enough, and you *won't* have the pleasure," answered Craig.

The man on the porch suddenly lifted the thick black veil of his lashes and gave Craig a glimpse of eyes strangely pale and bright. If this fellow was a dandy, he was something more, in addition. Craig was sure of it after one flash of those eyes. Suddenly he hesitated.

"Her pa's sick," said Craig. "Her pa's very sick, and she's gotta take care of him."

"I know her father is ill," said the stranger. "That's why I only ask a few seconds of her time, if you think that she can see me."

Craig hesitated, growling. Then he said that he would see, and went off to Ruth Wilbur. "There's a smart young fashion plate at the front door," he said. "Maybe you'd like to go and smile at him, eh? I guess he'd be ready to smile back!"

Ruth went to the door and found the dapper young man still waiting. His hat he tucked under his arm again, and he bowed at the sight of her. She pushed open, the screen door and told him to come in. He passed by her with an alert step so soundless that it startled her. He was not wearing rubber heels, either, for no dusty mark was left on the surface of the floor paint. He stood in the hall, bowing to her again. He had the supple grace of a fencer.

"Miss Wilbur," he said, "I've come to tell you that I'm a friend of the real Jim Silver, and I've learned what you did for him today. When I say that I'm a friend of Silver's, I mean that I'm a man whose life he has saved as surely as you saved his today. He's not out of trouble yet, but if he has a ghost of a chance, it's because you fought for him.

"I've come here to thank you. I'm not the only one. When the people know the whole truth, there are plenty of other friends of Silver scattered all through the mountains, and they'll all be ready to die for you. I've come to tell you, as the first of the lot, that if there's ever a thing that you need or if you're ever in trouble, I'll hear you whistle from the ends of the earth and come to help. My real name doesn't matter. People usually call me Taxi."

She thought it was a strange and simple speech, and it was given point by his name. She knew about Taxi, too. It surprised her to see that he was so young, because his was one of the great names in the legend of Jim Silver. And though Silver himself was not more than between twenty-eight and thirty-five, she never thought of him except as a hero gray with time. Taxi was the man, it was said, in whom Silver had more implicit faith than in any other person in the world.

She broke out: "I've heard that there's danger to him, now, from the town mob! What's to be done about it, Taxi? I don't need thanks for what I've done. The whole world owes something to the real Jim Silver. But tell me if it's possible that the crowd may smash the jail."

Taxi looked no higher than her hands. It was his habit, when he was talking with a person, unless that person was Jim Silver. He said:

"They've built a battering-ram that ought to be strong enough to beat in the doors of the jail. The town's full. People have come in from the whole countryside. The Easterners who have been taking the cure up in the hotel at the springs have rented window space overlooking the jail. Everybody seems to know for sure that there'll be a lynching party tonight."

"We've got to mix with the crowd and explain that it is not the robber that's now in the jail," said the girl. "We've got to explain to the sheriff, first of all."

"I've mixed with the crowd already," said Taxi, "and tried to make some suggestions like that, and I had to dodge a few punches and get away from a gun play. The people in this town are pretty much worked up, and they're not soothed by knowing that your father is a very sick man. They attribute that to Jim Silver, too, and they feel that they're in honor bound to make an end of the man in jail. Nothing can influence 'em. They're only waiting for night."

"Can we do nothing?" cried the girl.

"I'm going to try," said Taxi, "but my hand has to be played alone."

CHAPTER 19

Taxi's Lone Hand

Taxi walked up to the top of a hill that overlooked the town of Crow's Nest. He sat down on a rock and took out of his clothes the various parts of a little spyglass and screwed them together. It was small, like most of the tools that Taxi employed, but it had as fine a lens as money could buy.

First, he scanned the town with his naked eye, and glanced out of the wooded hollow that contained Crow's Nest to the profound depths of the valley beyond, now misting over with the shadows of the evening, like a slowly rising tide of thin water.

The glass changed all of this. He could penetrate the mists of the valley and see the sheen of the river that ran through the bottom lands, a bright, golden sheen as the sun walked farther down the bow of heaven toward the west. In the town itself he could pick out figures walking the streets, and presently he caught the jail itself in clear focus.

It was set in the midst of an open stretch. No other building was within half a block of it, and that was why he was able to see the cordon which had been drawn around the prison by the townsmen. There seemed to be three or four hundred already on the job. Traffic had been blocked. It was like an established battle line.

When he was sure of the setting, he examined the building itself. When the rest of the ground had been cleared, the builders had remembered the fierce heat of the summer, and they had allowed several big trees to stand close to the jail. The shadows of these, from the west, poured across the roof of the building, and it was only after much searching that he was able to detect the presence of the skylight. It was small, and it was hardly raised at all above the surface of the roof.

When Taxi was sure of that, he spent a few more minutes studying the windows of the jail as they appeared from this side, and the big door. Then he unscrewed the assembled spyglass and put it away in his clothes. The lens fitted into a velvet-lined, small pocket on the inside of his belt. He stood up, dusted his clothes with care, and then walked slowly down to the town.

He went into a restaurant, got a corner table, and ate a light meal. By the time he had finished, it was almost completely dark. He saw the big Negro dishwasher throw off his wet apron, grab a hat, and hurry out of the place. The cook followed. There was only the waiter remaining, and he seemed discontented to be left behind.

Taxi did not need to be told where the other pair were going. He left in his turn. He passed the local general merchandise store, which was kept open until eight o'clock for the convenience of such late shoppers as ranchers and lumberjacks. In that store he bought a length of rope and walked out with his purchase. In the first vacant lot he hid himself in a nest of shrubbery, pulled off his coat, and wound the rope around and around his body. Then he went on.

The next problem was to pass the cordon that was stretched around the jail. No one was allowed to go through, and a number of lanterns had been supplied, and, carrying them, men were constantly walking up and down the line. That was what gave Taxi his idea.

He found the source of the lantern supply at one corner of the cordon, where they were being filled and passed out. He saw a big fellow with a face made grim by a saber-shaped mustache, who seemed to be in charge of the lanterns. But without asking permission, Taxi filled one from the five-gallon kerosene can, trimmed the wick, and lighted it. Then he went off down the back of the crowded line of the cordon.

No one paid any attention to him until he turned through the line and walked straight across the open ground toward the jail. Instantly voices hailed him, then. "Who's that? Who's going there?"

Taxi turned around without haste.

"D'you think I'm going for fun?" he asked. At that remark someone laughed out loud.

"You fool," said another, "d'you think he'd be carrying a light to *show* himself if he was sneaking for the jail on any business except ours?"

That was apparently in answer to some suspicious suggestion. Taxi walked straight on, slowly, and more slowly, taking his leaping nerves in hand and forcing them to be quiet.

When he was very close to the jail, he simply turned down the wick, and with one jouncing movement of the lantern caused the flame to sicken and die.

The darkness that followed would hide him from the observation of the men of the cordon.

He turned down the side of the building until he came to the big trees at the western end of it. A spruce was the one he wanted, a grand fellow with wide, shaggy arms. He went up the trunk of that tree like a monkey. A wind was rising. The noise of it in the tree he climbed was like the rushing sound of the sea on a beach, and its noise in the neighboring trees was like the noise of distant beaches.

When he gained the top of the tree, he was well above the level of the roof of the jail. He could mark the dim outline of the skylight that projected a little above the roof line. It had seemed close to the trees, when he was looking down from the top of the hill. Now it seemed far away.

He took the rope, built a small noose in it, and suddenly wished for the skill that was possessed by ten thousand cowpunchers on the range. But that skill was not his, and he knew from experience of old what he would have to use as a substitute—patience.

That was what sustained him as, time and again, he made the cast from the treetop, and once in five times the noose would fall true over the little skylight, but every time, no matter how carefully he drew the rope taut, the noose slipped over the projection of the skylight, and his bag was emptiness.

Then a certain change in the voice of the crowd made his heart leap. There was not much that his eye could see, except a greater collection of people at one point in the cordon, and an assembling of lanterns, there. Those lanterns did not flash on the pallor of shining faces; he saw that the crowd, at least in this section, had been masked. That meant that the ringleaders had appeared on the scene, that the striking force had been assembled, and that the assault on the jail would presently follow.

Taxi climbed down the tree, found half a dozen small stones, and tied them to one side of the noose of the rope. Then he returned to the top of the tree, and made the cast. The stones fell with a distinctly audible thud on the roof near the skylight. How the noose had flopped he could not be sure, but he hoped that it had fallen down the slope of the roof, over the skylight and that the weight of the little stones would hold the rope flat until the drawn noose caught on something.

Gingerly he drew in on the rope, little by little, like a fisherman most delicately playing a small fish. Then from beneath him and around the corner of the jail, he heard the pounding of a hand against the door.

"Hey, Sheriff Williams! Hey, Dick!" called a voice. "I wanta talk to you!"

Then a voice, half hollow from confinement inside the building and half freely issuing into the night, rejoined: "I know you, Nick, I know your voice. I hope that you ain't mixed up in this rotten business."

"Dick," said Nick, "I'm mixed up in it, all right. We want the dirty crook and bank robber, Jim Silver. We want the rat who smashed the bank and killed Henry Wilbur, and we're goin' to have him."

"Is Wilbur dead?" cried the sheriff.

"He's pretty nigh to it. If he ain't dead, it ain't the fault of Jim Silver. Dick, don't you be a fool now."

"I ain't a fool," said the sheriff. "I just got a job to do, and I'm goin' to do it."

"Dick," urged the other, "you know me very well and you know that I don't go in for crooked work, don't you?"

"You're in a crooked deal if you try to smash this jail," said the sheriff, "and I'll have you in the pen for your share in it—if I live to talk tomorrow."

"It's a thing that maybe you ain't sure to do," said Nick grimly. "I'm telling you, man to man, that we got this jail like a nut in a nutcracker. We can split it open any time we want to. The boys are spoiling for action, and they're going to have it."

"You tell the boys," shouted the sheriff, "that if they try to rush this jail, I'll open up on 'em, and that I'll shoot to kill."

There was a pause. Then: "Dick, do you think Jim Silver is guilty?"

"I ain't a fool," said the sheriff. "I know that he's as guilty as anything."

"You know the talk they're makin' about a false Jim Silver, a counterfeit Jim Silver—you know that that is fool talk, don't you?"

"Sure it's fool talk," agreed the sheriff, "but that don't mean that I'm goin' to let you boys have what you want."

"Dick, will you kill honest men to keep them from lynching a dirty, bank-robbing crook?"

"I'll do my duty—that's certain!" shouted Dick Williams, and a window slammed shut.

CHAPTER 20

Inside the Jail

Time was short. Oh, time was very short indeed. When Nick brought the sheriff's final answer back to the crowd, there might be an instant rush for the jail. The whole mob might break loose in a mighty wave.

Taxi pulled in on his rope. It seemed to catch, then it slipped. He groaned as he made sure that it had failed once more, but then he found it holding again. He put his weight on the rope, and still it held, trembling with tautness.

At last he ventured on tying it fast around the trunk of the tree and swinging out along the rope. The treetop instantly swayed far over. He found himself in the bight of the rope, hauling himself uphill toward the edge of the roof.

Now his grip was on the eaves, and soon he was on the roof. The tree, springing back, released from the strain, caused the rope to snap against him, almost knocking him off his feet.

Then he discovered that the rope was not holding by the edges of the skylight. It had caught on a single nail that was half buried in the edge of the window frame. He took one deep breath as he thought of what might have happened; then he fell to work on the lock of the skylight.

The glass was heavy, very thick, and very strong. Nevertheless, he worked a glass cutter noiselessly through it, cut out a hand hole, and pulled back the spring lock. After that he raised the skylight and cut into the darkness beneath him with a few slashing strokes of his flashlight. It showed to him a long and empty attic room, with a low ceiling and naked rafters. There were some dust-covered boxes here and there. That was the only furniture.

Taxi went down the rough wooden steps from the skylight to the attic floor. Out of the darkness of that floor he could see a single thin ray of light standing up like a polished rapier. He came to the hole in the floor and put his eye to the crack. The whole cell room lay beneath him. He was in the exact center of the big room, lying on top of a trap-door which opened down.

With one hand he took off his shoes, as he stared. It was just the sort of a picture that he had expected. There were two blocks of the little steel cells, and two aisles that ran between them. In each of those aisles, armed with a sawed-off shotgun, a guard was striding up and down. The sheriff sat in a chair at the front of the room, nervously smoking a cigar. Now and again he jumped up and walked a few steps, peered down one or the other of the aisles, and returned to his chair again.

After a moment he came up to the guard who slouched up and down the aisle, just below Taxi.

"How's things, Pete?" he asked.

The guard halted and swung his shotgun to the hook of his left arm. He settled one hand flat on the hip of the overalls which covered him.

"How do I know how things are?" he asked, and then jerked the brim of his big slouch hat still lower over his eyes. "Things are the way the gents outside are gain' to make 'em," he declared.

The sheriff nodded.

"Keep your eye on Silver," he added. "There ain't anybody else in this aisle to bother you. There's only Silver. Keep watching his hands and see that the irons are always on him. He's a tricky devil."

"There ain't any trick in the world as good as the buckshot that I poured into this here gun and stopped up with wadding," said the guard, patting the double barrels of the shotgun. "I got enough in each barrel to wash a whole crowd off a street!" He laughed with a long, drawling, nasal intonation of joy in his voice.

The sheriff looked him up and down curiously.

"I kinda think you *hope* that the gang breaks in here and tries to rush you, Pete," he suggested.

"I ain't sayin' nothin', but I've shot a pile of ducks in my day," remarked Pete.

The smile of the sheriff was turned to a grimace by a deep, muttering uproar that started outside the jail and swept more and more loudly through the air.

"They're coming!" said the sheriff. "I'm going into the office and see what things are like on that side. Pete, it may be guns and a fight to the finish, for all I know."

He turned and was gone, running. Pete looked after him for a moment, and then slowly strode up the length of the aisle, paused to stare into the one cell whose door was shut, and then went gradually on.

It was Taxi's moment, and he used it by opening the catch that secured the trap-door and letting it hang down. He himself was instantly through the opening, hanging from the under edge of the swinging door. Luckily the hinges did not creak. Then he dropped, and there was only the softest of thudding sounds as his stockinged feet struck the cement floor.

The guard was already at the far end of the aisle, where he half turned to the side and said to the man who paced the next aisle: "The soup's goin' to be hot pretty soon."

"Yeah, pretty hot, pretty soon," said the other guard.

"Hope you don' t burn your tongue on it," remarked Pete, and chuckled.

Taxi, in the meantime, was gliding rapidly up the aisle, and there, to his left, behind the bars of the closed cell in the center of the block of cells, he saw Jim Silver.

The big man was sitting on the edge of his cot, his legs, his arms, loaded with irons. As Taxi went by, the great head lifted a little. That was all. But Taxi saw the sheen of the eyes and the glint of light on the gray spots above the temples of the prisoner. Those spots looked more like horns than ever.

Pete, finishing his conversation, started to turn back to resume his beat. As he turned, Taxi, leaping the last of the distance, struck with the heel of his gun. It was not the first time he had bludgeoned a man, and he knew the force required to knock a man flat without shattering the skull.

He used the right force now, but, to his amazement, Pete did not fall. He only took one half-step back, and braced himself, the shotgun starting to slip out of his hands.

Taxi snatched that gun away. He raised the automatic to strike with the heel of it again, and then he saw that the eyes of the guard were totally lifeless. The man was unconscious on his feet.

Taxi rammed a shoulder against Pete's stomach and folded him over like a half-filled sack. Then, almost running, he returned to the cell of Jim Silver. At the same time, from the outside of the jail, the growing wave of uproar washed suddenly around the building.

Taxi spilled the guard to the floor and thrust his picklock into the keyhole of the cell door. They might be very difficult, those locks. He heard the sheriff shouting from the front part of the jail, perhaps threatening the crowd. In the whirling brain of Taxi there was no chance to sort out the sounds and recognize the words.

Now the bolt yielded, suddenly, and the door was open. He flung the guard inside, caught at the irons on the wrists of Silver.

"It's a bad lock, Taxi," said Silver. "It'll take time to do it."

Taxi stifled a groan behind the click of his teeth. If he needed time, there was only one way to get it. He turned to the guard, stripped the overalls from the limp body, and jumped into them. They covered his own clothes from head to foot. The boots of Pete were big and loose. He had them off and on his own feet instantly, jammed the slouch hat of Pete on his head, caught up the shotgun, and, tossing his automatic to Silver, stepped out into the aisle.

That instant the office door was flung open, and the sheriff rushed out, shouting: "They've got a big battering-ram, boys! They're goin' to beat down the front door. I can't find it in my heart to shoot at 'em! I can't murder 'em because they want to hang a crook!"

"Bird shot!" called the other guard. "Give 'em bird shot, Dick."

"There ain't any bird shot, you fool!" cried the sheriff.

The moment he was out of view, Taxi turned back into the cell. He dropped to his knees and began to toil at the lock of the handcuffs. Seconds counted. Every second might be the end of it all, and yet he could not hurry. He had to take hold of himself with the full grasp of his will. He had to control himself as though he were frozen to attention, listening to a very distant sound.

As a matter of fact, he kept himself oblivious of the uproar around him. The batteringram struck its first blow against the front door of the jail. The whole building seemed to quiver with the weight of the stroke. There was a sound of splintering wood.

With a tenth part of his mind, Taxi heard that telltale sound and registered the meaning of it. Then the handcuffs sprang open!

"Good work! Wonderful work! Back into the aisle for a breather," said the calm voice of Jim Silver.

What a man was that! The calm for which Taxi had to fight with hysterical intentness was merely the gift of God to Jim Silver. There was not a tremor in his body that Taxi could feel. His hand under the manacle had been steady as a stone.

"The leg irons another time," said Silver. "Leave me the picklock. I may be able to work them."

Taxi gave him the picklock and stepped out into the aisle again. He was only the flicker of an eyelash ahead of the reappearance of the sheriff, who shouted to him:

"This way, Pete. Help me hold 'em at the door."

Taxi, turning his back, walked resolutely down the aisle. He tried to force the nasal drawl of Pete into his voice as he shouted in answer:

"My job's here, and here's where I stay."

"You stubborn fool!" yelled the sheriff. Then he turned and fired a revolver bullet through the upper part of the big door. There was a great outcry and a scrambling of feet and stamping outside, on the steps.

"Keep away from that door, or I'll drill some of you!" yelled Dick.

Then through the crack of the door a voice came booming, half stifled: "Williams, if you fire another shot, we're goin' to pull you apart and break your wishbone in two. Don't be a fool!"

Taxi was already back in the cell with his friend, for Silver had abandoned the little picklock to him with a despairing shake of the head.

On the floor, Pete was beginning to stir and groan softly.

CHAPTER 21

The Mob

Dick Williams, frantic with fear and excitement, and savage with desire to do his duty, was yelling from the front of the jail that he would let a streak of light into the first man who dared to dash open the front door of the building, when there was a sudden heavy crash against the rear door of the jail. The mob had wrecked the front entrance so that a child could knock down the flimsy ruin that remained standing. Now it had gone behind the jail and was splintering the rear door. They yelled in rhythm and chorus as they swung the heavy timber that served them as a battering-ram.

The sheriff, when he heard this new outbreak, began to turn around in a blind and helpless circle, crying out orders where there were no men to help him perform the work in hand.

Taxi, in this moment, had made Jim Silver free. Instead of an incubus, he had loosed a force that would be felt far away, and before long. From the fallen guard, Silver took a pair of revolvers that Taxi had not searched for. As that unlucky Pete recovered his wits, Silver was saying to him:

"Wait thirty seconds, Pete. Then you can make all the noise you want."

Silver then stepped behind Taxi into the open aisle of the jail and closed the door behind him. Forward, Taxi saw Dick Williams shooting through the top of the front door of the jail.

"That way!" said Taxi to his friend, and pointed toward the little trap-door that hung from the ceiling. How they would get through it he could not tell. Better brains and stronger hands than his own could struggle with the problem now. Silver went forward at a halting run, measured his distance, bounded high, and caught the trap-door with his hands. He swung like a pendulum through half a vibration, shifted his grip higher, and now hung from the edge of the attic floor. He was through the opening in a moment, and now he appeared, hanging down from the waist, his long arms dangling, his hands in the air, reaching far down.

"Jump, Taxi!" he called quietly.

Taxi knew that he could not reach the lower tip of the trap-door, but it was an easy jump for him to catch hold of the hands of Silver. The force of his leap swung him backward and forward, while the voice of Pete, the guard, went yelling through the jail:

"Dick! Dick! Hi, Dick Williams! The devil's come and took Jim Silver away!"

Dick Williams had something else to think about, for the rear door of the jail went down with a crash as Taxi's body disappeared through the trap in the ceiling, drawn strongly upward by Jim Silver's grasp. The door itself Silver closed again and left the lower floor of the jail to the guards who had been set to keep him for the law, and the mob which had come to hang him with its own hands. Silver could not help smiling a little when he considered how perfectly Taxi had performed the impossible and caused him to disappear at the crucial moment.

It was a proof that Jim Silver did not need, a certainty that the affection of Taxi would endure while there was breath in his body.

They were fumbling in the darkness toward the stairs that led up to the skylight. Beneath them the building roared and shook with the entrance of the mob. Outside of the building the angry men of the town were gathered. Certainly the two were far from safe, but they were together, and, therefore, the strength of each was multiplied; they were armed, and the terrible hands of Jim Silver were free.

"They'll be after us as fast as they can fetch a ladder to the trap-door," said Taxi. "But I've got a bridge that may snake us off the roof."

"A bridge into what?" asked Silver. "Into the sky?"

They came out onto the roof. Above them, the sky was closely powdered with the stars; below them down the sharp slant of the roof, they could see the whole male population of Crow's Nest swarming in to take part in the lynching, or to be witnesses of it. Lanterns tossed here and there, and long yellow splashes of light streaked across the roof. If the two men on top of the jail were not seen, it was only because no eyes thought of looking up there.

At the edge of the skylight, Taxi said: "Here's the rope. Wait till I fasten it around the door, then swing along it to the tree, Jim. This is the way I got to the jail."

His flying hands had already reached down into the skylight and noosed the rope around the door. "Go first," said Silver.

"'No, no! It's you that they want. They wouldn't stretch my neck, Jim. You're the bird they're after."

"Go first," said the calm voice of Silver.

Taxi gave him one despairing glance. But he knew that there was no use arguing against that unruffled insistence. He slipped off the edge of the roof, worked down the slack of the rope to the bight of it, and began to hand over hand himself up the farther end to the tree.

As he went, he had glimpses of the crowd below. It seemed to him that all the faces were turned up toward him. The black masks on them made them like figures in a dream, those misty countenances that never can be resolved into features, mere blank sketches of the imagination.

One thing more he saw in the distance, in the middle of the street, and that was the shining picture of Parade. It was strange that he should have been led out, as though it were part of the cruel plan of the mob to make the poor horse see the death of his master. But there he stood, with his head high and his tail arching, looking apart from the crowd and free of it and above it in the perfection of his beauty.

Now, in the dark of the tree, Taxi reached the trunk, looked down through the branches, made sure that no one had, in fact, marked his escape, and jerked several times on the slack of the rope to let Silver know that the way was open.

It was high time, for the uproar in the jail was rising upward in it, a sure sign that a ladder had been placed already against the trap. Now and then a gun exploded, but it was plain that no violence had been used on Dick Williams or the guards. Taxi had time to be glad of that, and then he saw the big form of Silver come swinging across the rope, the top of the tree bending far over, the slack of the rope hanging down in a deep loop.

A moment more and he was among the branches. He was safe for the present, clinging to the trunk of the spruce tree. The rope, unknotted, swung outward and dangled like a great snake down the side of the jail.

"Masks! Masks!" called Silver. "Your coat lining, Taxi!"

It was like Silver to remember every detail even in the pinch of fast action. Taxi ripped out a great section of lining from the back of his coat, thrust his thumb through it twice to make eyeholes, and put the cloth over his head. It made a sufficient mask, though a clumsy one. Glancing up, he saw that Silver had completed his preparations before him and was now descending.

Taxi went down the trunk of the tree, hung from the lowest branch an instant, and then dropped to the ground. Hands were instantly gripping him. "Who are you?" shouted a voice at his ear.

"Silver's on the roof of the jail!" cried Taxi. "Think I'd stay there in the tree till I was shot out of it like a partridge? Silver's on the roof of the jail!"

"The roof!" yelled the men around Taxi, instantly letting him go. "Silver's on the roof of the jail!"

They gave back, scattering this way and that, preparing their guns to fire at random at any target.

Jim Silver himself slid down the trunk of the tree and stepped beside Taxi.

"Now!" said Silver, as they edged away through the thick of the crowd. "Where's your horse?"

"Tied to a hitch rack a block from here."

"Go get him. Which way?"

"First turn to the right, next to the main street."

"Go get your horse."

"And what'll you do for a horse, Jim?"

"They can't keep Parade," said Silver. "Not after he hears me whistle. He'll come through them like a wind through dead leaves. Hurry, Taxi. These fellows are beginning to go wild."

It was true, for just now the manhunters who had climbed up through the attic of the jail came out on the roof and were dimly seen from the ground. A number of men raised their guns to shoot, until it was made out that there were not merely two, but a whole stream of men issuing from the skylight. Voices yelled back and forth from the ground to the roof. Advice was given; oaths went barking through the night. And then the whole body of the men who had first entered the jail began to swarm out of it.

Taxi already had wormed his way through the crowd; now he walked rapidly toward the place where he had left the mustang.

He could bless the mask that covered his face, for there were men carrying lanterns everywhere.

When Taxi had reached his mustang, he was instantly in the saddle and rode back to the corner from which he could see the throng around the stallion. People were shouting from the direction of the jail: "Saddle! Saddle! Get your horses, boys. Silver's gone. Watch Parade!"

There was sense in that, because every man of the lot knew that Jim Silver would sooner leave his right arm behind him than the great stallion.

Off on the edge of the sidewalk, wrapped in a cloak and staring toward the jail, Taxi saw Ruth Wilbur standing quietly.

Then, shrilling over the thicker, heavier noises of the crowd, Taxi heard the signal whistle of Jim Silver. It rang like a bugle call in the soul of Taxi, because he had heard that summons before. It almost caused him to turn the head of his horse and drive straight toward the point from which the signal had come. But he knew that that call was not for him, now.

It was the call for Parade, and the big horse suddenly went mad. He became the center of a whirling tumult. Men yelled in terror as he tried to get at them with his heels and his teeth. And suddenly he was fleeing with two ropes flinging out from his neck, uselessly. If only one of those ropes did not become entangled with his legs and drop him like a shot!

"Kill the horse!" yelled someone. "Silver's only half himself without his horse! Kill Parade!"

But that was not so easy. Parade ran dodging through the crowd, and it would have taken a sure and daring hand to fire at him without fear of sending the bullet into human flesh. Yet there were actually shots fired, and Taxi's heart stood still. It was as if he were watching a human running the gantlet, instead of the flight of a horse.

Then, on the verge of the crowd, the whistle sounded again. A big, panther-swift man leaped into the saddle, flattened along the back of the stallion, and sent Parade racing straight for the corner where Taxi waited. It came to Taxi, as an afterthought, that he was a partner in that flight. He pulled his mustang around and spurred; together they rushed down the dusty length of the street.

CHAPTER 22

Two Fugitives

Duff Gregor felt like a boy who has stolen a great wedge of pie and does not know where to bite into the treasure.

Barry Christian was taking a siesta in the cool entrance shaft of the old deserted mine which was the hiding place of the pair since they had fled from Crow's Nest. Duff Gregor, seated on the side of the old, grass-grown dump of the mine, looked over the heads of the pine trees down the mountain slope to the flash of creek water near which they had buried one of the canvas sacks of the treasure. The other sack they had sunk in the floor of the first shaft that branched to the left of the entrance.

It seemed to Gregor that he was seated on a throne from which he could view half the world. He could see the river in the bottom of the valley into which the creek flowed. He could see the smudge of distant smoke which announced the existence of the town of Sawmills. He could see the thin span of the bridge that crossed the river above the waterfalls. He could see the road that wound up through the green valley bottom.

It was a world in which the fools labored, and the wise men, like Duff Gregor and Barry Christian, sat on thrones and looked at the ant-like toil of lesser humans, now and again descending from their higher level to take away some of the accretions of wealth which the poor drudges had heaped up.

It was a delightful existence, thought Duff Gregor. It was for this that man was designed and made strong, with two hands equipped for snatching away the spoils of lesser folk. It was delightful, and it was kingly. Duff Gregor was new to a throne, but he felt that the role would grow increasingly natural to him. He only needed robes.

He could tell what those robes would be—long-tailed coats and white shirt fronts, with white ties and the great, rich flash of a jewel, here and there. In his ears, in his blood, there was continually running, not the music of mountain winds and mountain waters, but the song of violins and the whispering of feet over the floors of ballrooms. It seemed to Duff Gregor that he had always had a way with women. Now he wanted to use it, politely, in the best society. He felt that he knew just how to overwhelm the feminine brain by his free spending.

When he had finished surveying the world before him, this world which he was about to leave for the joy of great cities, he turned his attention to the newspaper which was a portion of the spoils that Barry Christian had brought back from his raid of the night before.

When they needed either provisions or information, they raided, not together but singly, because they felt that it would be a shame if both of them should be captured, and all of the good money from the bank in Crow's Nest be left to rot for many years in the ground. They would go down singly, therefore, and bring back from their excursions all the information that they could pick up, together with necessary provisions. For, though in retirement, they lived very well up here at the entrance to the old mine.

The mountains, though it was many days since the robbery of the bank, continued to be filled with searching parties, for the rage of the people against "Jim Silver" passed all bounds.

That was the beauty of the affair. That was what the masterful brain of Barry Christian had provided. They had committed a crime, they had "inherited" a fortune, and all they needed to do in order to escape from the dangers of the pursuit was to step back into their old selves. That is to say, all they needed was to make this change as soon as the public excitement had abated a little. Soon the little toiling parties of manhunters would no longer be observed from the aerie, and then the two could drift away into the larger world of men and be seen no more.

Christian was especially fond of referring to honest men as the "ants," and he called the hunting parties the "soldiers." Gregor smiled, as he thought of that, and shaking out the newspaper, he scanned the headlines with a calm eye of interest.

It was the Crow's Nest *Sentinel* that Christian had brought, and it was still crammed with details that concerned the great bank robbery. It pleased Gregor to find the phrase "great bank robbery." The crime was historical. It would never be forgotten. It was a monumental affair both on account of its size and because of the skill with which the criminals had worked. It was, in short, a perfect bit of work, and to be connected with such an event was worth some years in prison, even.

"Was Jim Silver the Robber?" said the top headline, in red letters. The article below it read:

Was Jim Silver the robber?

If so, who were the two men who were hunted out of Crow's Nest immediately after the crime and who were almost overtaken in the act of riddling with bullets the shack five miles from Crow's Nest where the celebrated character, Taxi, was fighting for his life?

Would Jim Silver permit an attack on Taxi, his best friend, his most celebrated admirer and faithful follower?

If Jim Silver robbed the bank, would he have been foolish enough to re-enter the town immediately after the crime was committed? Common sense tells us that this could not be.

People are ready to swear, now, that the man who was jailed in Crow's Nest for the crime and who was delivered by the frantic devotion and the incredible daring and skill of Taxi was, in fact, not the man who had been employed as watchman at the bank.

Miss Ruth Wilbur, who risked her life to save the poor fellow from the hands of the crowd, vows that it was not the same man. There are many others willing to swear to the dissimilarity, now. Unfortunately, on the day of the excitement they did not dare to lift their voices because the majority of the citizens were too enraged to listen to calm reason.

It seems that we have been hoaxed by a cunning actor who "doubled" for the famous Jim Silver. If so, how can the injustice be undone?

Hundreds or even thousands of men are working through the mountains in an attempt to spot the criminals. Will they be able to tell the real from the unreal?

We need the real Jim Silver to help us find the false one. But could the real Jim Silver venture back to offer his services to us without running the risk of being shot down at a distance?

The whole affair is confused, and in the meantime every moment that passes makes it more and more unlikely that the two desperadoes will be apprehended. Certainly they must have found means of disposing of most of their stolen wealth before this day.

Duff Gregor read over this article several times. He licked his lips as he read.

There were other things in the paper to which he gave a more casual attention. There was the notice at length, for instance, that Henry Wilbur, the banker, having almost entirely recovered from his collapse on the morning of the robbery, was pushing ahead plans for the sale of all his property in order to pay back what promised to be about ninety cents on the dollar to every depositor in the bank.

There was a long editorial comment on the nobility of Mr. Wilbur's action, and the editor remarked that Mr. Wilbur was not really a banker at all, but the father of his community, preferring to surrender his own welfare to that of his children.

Duff Gregor grinned.

Barry Christian, he felt, was entirely right. They were just ants, those others. The little spot of their labors was their entire existence, and one of them would shed his precious blood to secure the good of the community.

His thought drifted from Henry Wilbur to the character of the banker's daughter, and at this point Duff Gregor's self-content began to rub thin.

He said, finally: "Aw, it ain't the first time that I was a fool! I'll forget it, like I forgot the other times." Lifting his eyes from the newspaper, he looked down into the bottom of the valley and became aware that there was a scene of violent action down there. Yes, there was a faint, far sound, smaller than the noise of bees, and it was composed of the rattle of firearms.

Two men were being chased up the valley by more than thirty riders, and one of the fugitives was mounted upon a horse that shone like gold.

"It ain't Jim Silver. It *can't* be Jim Silver," said Duff Gregor to himself.

He snatched out a pair of field glasses and peered through the strong lenses until the scene was drawn up closer to him. Then he was sure. He was sure not only because he could see more of the matchless running of the golden horse, but he could understand why it was that so patently glorious an animal did not draw away from the hunt. It was because the rider preferred to risk his own neck by returning again and again to defend his companion, who was not nearly so well-mounted.

That companion was a smaller man and he was riding like a jockey, bent far forward in the saddle; but though his weight must have been slight, still he could not draw away from the best riders of the pursuit. They would have closed in on him like hounds on a tired deer, had it not been that the rider of the golden horse turned back time after time and opened fire on the posse with his rifle.

Each time, the posse fanned out, scattered, and returned the bullets with a great, random spread of fire. But always the daring hero on the golden horse swung away again, unharmed.

"Barry! Barry!" called Duff Gregor. "Come out here!"

"What's the matter?" asked the sleepy voice of Christian, from inside the mine.

"There's a thing out here that'll do you more good than anything else you ever seen in your life," answered Gregor. "Come out here and take a look."

"Whatever it is, it's not worth spoiling my sleep," said Christian angrily. "Duff, will you ever grow up and have sense?"

"Is that so?" answered Gregor.

"That's exactly what I mean."

"You wouldn't come out here and look, I suppose," said Gregor, "if Jim Silver and Taxi were down there in the hollow, being run to death by about thirty gents?"

"Don't bother me," answered Christian.

"Because," shouted the other, "that's exactly what's happening down there, or else I'm blind as a bat and a fool besides."

Christian, suddenly, stood beside him, gave one glance into the green hollow of the valley, and then snatched the field glasses. He held them in his steady hand for only an instant before he exclaimed:

"You're right. And it *is* Jim Silver. The other fellow—can that be Taxi? Duff, am I going to see the end of both of 'em on one day?"

CHAPTER 23

The Gambling Chance

Duff Gregor stared with incredulous joy. "You know Silver by the horse," he exclaimed, "but what makes you sure of Taxi? You *ain't* sure!"

Christian answered as he followed with his eyes the action in the valley beneath him, saying:

"There comes the wave of 'em after Taxi! He's turning around to fight back. He can't run any more on that dead-beat horse. Now Silver comes sweeping back to him. He waves his arm at Silver to send him away. What man in the world would do that except a fool like Taxi? He's waving Silver away, but Silver comes on in between Taxi and the posse—and the posse scatters. Why do the fools scatter?"

"Why shouldn't they scatter?" asked Duff Gregor. "Ain't Silver the sort that doesn't know how to miss?"

No matter how interested he was in the moving picture beneath them, Christian was too annoyed by the last remark of his companion to let it pass. He lowered the field glasses suddenly and turned his handsome face toward Duff Gregor.

"Gregor," he said, "you know something about Jim Silver, and you've heard a good deal about him from me. Don't you understand that the law-abiding are as safe from him as sheep are from a sheep dog? If that were a mob of thugs riding up the valley after him, or if your own precious person were in the lot, you can be sure that his bullets would be biting flesh long before this. But those fools are riding on behalf of the law, as they think, and they're perfectly safe from him. They ought to know it—but they won't know it. They've got their own ideas and they'll stick by them."

He clapped the glasses back to his eyes again. Then he laughed.

"Silver's shooting the gravel away in front of their horses. He's kissing the air beside their heads. I can see them duck. Now Taxi and Silver are running for it again."

He lowered the glasses a second time as the fugitives passed into a dark cloud of trees. The posse men herded in pursuit.

"They've got 'em!" exclaimed Duff Gregor. "That's the end of Mr. Jim Silver. That's the end of Taxi, too. That's the finish of the pair of 'em."

He observed that Christian was shaking his head, slowly, with an air of grave doubt.

"Come on, Barry," urged Gregor. "What else can happen? Silver is too crazy to leave Taxi. Taxi's horse is dead spent, and a lot of those horses in the posse look full of running. They've got fifteen to one. How can they fail to catch Silver and Taxi?"

"I don't know," said Christian. "It simply isn't in the books."

Gregor started to laugh, but something of suffering and a sternness of pain in the face of Barry Christian dried up the mirth on his lips.

"Listen, Barry," said Gregor. "Are you believing what you say?"

"Silver can't be run down like a dog. A lot of house dogs can't run down a wolf like Jim Silver," said Christian. "When he dies, it'll be because another sort of man has come to grips with him."

"A man like Barry Christian?" hazarded Gregor suddenly.

"Well, perhaps."

"D'you think that you are fated to wipe Jim Silver off the face of the earth?" asked Gregor, half sneering.

Christian looked at him without anger, answering: "I don't think a great deal about it. It's simply a feeling in my bones that one day Silver will be the death of me or I'll be the death of him."

"Why, it's working out like that now," declared Gregor. "You do a big job and saddle the blame of it on Silver, and the crowd runs him down. It's your work that's finishing off Jim Silver right down there in the pines."

Christian answered: "You don't understand. When the finish comes, we'll be hand to hand. I don't even think that there'll be knives or guns. Just hand to hand!"

He turned his right hand palm up and looked down at it. This curious mood of detachment, Gregor had observed in his famous companion more than once before this, and it always troubled him. There were times when it seemed that Christian was listening to unearthly voices, and this was one of the times.

Christian began to walk up and down before the mine, deep in thought, and Duff Gregor followed him with a calculating eye. Trouble, he felt, was in the air. He was not surprised when he heard Christian say:

"Well, we'll have to get out of this."

"You don't mean that we're going to move?" demanded Gregor.

"Why not?"

"Why not? Because we' re perfectly fixed, up here. Nobody dreams that we're staying put like this. Nobody thinks that we're tucked away with all that money in a hole in the ground. We're fixed here, Barry. We're safe. We'd be fools if we stirred away from here before we had to!"

Christian looked far away, and shook his head. "I don't like it!" he said.

"You don't like what?"

"Silver. He's too near us. If he's as near as that, he'll get the wind of us."

"How can he do that?"

"I don't know. Don't ask me how Silver does things. Ask me how he got out of jail when a mob was trying to lynch him."

"Why, Taxi did that job."

"All right. But it was more impossible for him to get out of that jail than it is for him to find us."

"Barry," said Gregor suddenly, "tell me something. Are you afraid of Silver?" Christian pointed solemnly at the sky.

"Are you afraid of lightning?" he asked.

"Yeah. But what's that got to do with it?" demanded Gregor.

"I don't know. I feel about Silver the way I do about lightning. That's all. I feel that he may strike at any time. He's near us. We've got to move."

"It's a crazy thing to do," groaned Gregor, knowing that he would have to give way to his leader. "When do we start?"

"Now," said Christian.

"Now? Right out in the broad daylight, where these manhunters can get a look at us?"

"The day helps the other fellow to see you, but it also helps you to see the other fellow. We'd better start now."

Duff Gregor snapped his fingers and whistled to express the wordless vastness of his condemnation of the proposal.

"It's the craziest thing that I ever heard of," he declared. "I never heard anything to beat it. Listen to me, Barry. I'll tell you what we'll do. We'll toss a coin to see whether we start now or at moonrise tonight."

"All right," said Christian. "Toss the coin."

He smiled a little as he said it, for he knew that Gregor was fond of appealing to the deathless love of the gambling chance that was part of Christian's nature.

Gregor pulled out a coin and threw it high into the air. At the top of its rise it hung for an instant, spinning so fast that it was reduced to a single twinkling eye of light.

"Heads," said Christian.

The coin came down with a spat on the flat of the ground. Christian and Gregor leaned over it.

"All right," said Christian. "We start at moonrise."

"It's better that way, isn't it?" Gregor said.

Christian shrugged his big shoulders as he said: "I don't know. There's something like frost working in my blood. But let's forget it."

So they forgot about it. At least, Christian seemed to have abandoned all care about the future, for he stretched out and slumbered heavily during most of the day. Gregor observed him with a good deal of awe and envy. He could understand that sheer power of will had enabled Christian to abandon fear for the time being and discard all forethought. So Christian slept, and Gregor daydreamed of the future, until sunset.

In that hour between day and dark Christian wakened and with Gregor ate a cold supper. He absolutely refused to light even the smallest of fires for fear that either the smoke or the red eye of the blaze should be seen.

The sunset colors went out. The mountains stood like black islands, for a time, in a sea of fading green. Then the night shut closely in. The stars burned lower and lower until they reached their full brightness, and not long after, the moon rose.

They had brought the horses up out of the mine, before this, and saddled them and rolled their blankets. Now they tethered the pair to a sapling and went down the hill to get the canvas sack of treasure which they had buried near the bank of the creek.

The nerves of Christian were so finely strung, by this time, that he stopped short when a twig crackled a little distance up the slope. "What's the matter?" asked Gregor.

"Hush!" whispered Christian. "Something alive stepped on a twig, up there. A man?"

"Men ain't the only things that walk through the wood," answered Gregor. "Don't get nervous, Barry."

He wondered at himself, giving advice like that to a creature made of steel springs, like Christian.

Still, for a long moment, Christian listened. He stood where a spot of moonlight struck him through the branches of a pine; now he shifted out of this light, making no noise as he stirred. At last he murmured:

"All right. We'll go ahead. But keep your ears open."

They went on down to the bank of the creek, where the moonlight broke through the shrubbery in the midst of which they had buried the first canvas sack. Christian had brought down from the mine the same broken-handled shovel with which he had dug the hole in the first place. The earth turned easily, but as the hole opened, and he drove the shovel blade strongly down, he uttered a faint exclamation of astonishment.

"What's the matter?" asked Gregor.

In place of answering, Christian fell to work digging furiously. After a few moments he stopped. Gregor could hear him panting, but more than the sound of the heavy breathing was the sight of the long-barreled Colt that was leveled at him suddenly in the moonlight.

"You know what's the matter, you thieving dog!" said Christian. "You've stolen the sack away from this place!"

CHAPTER 24

Missing Loot

Gregor stared at the hole in the ground and then at the gun, lifted his eyes last of all to the set, grim face of Barry Christian. He knew that there was as little mercy in the soul of that man as in a piece of hard-tempered steel.

"Stolen?" gasped Gregor. "The sack stolen? Gimme the shovel!"

He took the shovel and fell to work furiously, enlarging and deepening the excavation until the shovel began to bite into the clay hardpan. Then he stepped away from his work with a groan.

"Not possible!" said Gregor.

"Possible? Anything's possible for a rat with a yellow, sneaking heart!" said Christian. "Now just double-quick to the place where you hid the stuff out for yourself."

The brain of Gregor spun.

"But I didn't touch it. I don't know where it is," he said.

"You *will* know in a minute," said Christian. "Do your thinking while I count to ten. You can stop me any time by telling me that you remember."

"Barry," said the other, "are you clean out of your head, man? If I wanted to get everything for myself, I could have brained you today while you were asleep."

"You know I sleep light," answered Christian.

"Do you think I would have stood by here," said Gregor, "knowing you were digging down to something that wouldn't be there and that you'd accuse me of stealing? Barry, man, have sense. I could have filled you with lead while you were digging the hole just now."

Christian hesitated, as though he hated to believe what he heard or give up the grim purpose which had already hardened his mind.

At last he said: "There's something in what you say."

"Of course there is. There's everything in it," groaned Gregor, sighing with relief.

"Then who could have taken it?" demanded Christian.

"The devil, for all I know," said Gregor. "It's the craziest thing that I ever heard."

"The name of the devil is Jim Silver," said Christian, "and he can hardly have been here. But the woods are full of soft-footed mountaineers, all eyes and ears. One of 'em might have seen us bury the stuff. In that case, he'd just dig up the loot and cart it away. Of course, he wouldn't inform the sheriff."

"But why should he fill in the hole again?" asked Gregor.

"So that we wouldn't start looking for his trail, if we happened down here soon to look at the spot where the stuff was hidden," said Christian.

"Aye, and that must be it," admitted Gregor. "That's it, and little good it does us!"

They stared at one another. Slowly, with small, jerky, uneasy moves, Christian put away the gun. There had been murder in his mind, and it was hard for him to discard the temptation in a single gesture. If a killing were to be done, Gregor knew that Christian would go about it as calmly and as methodically as he had gone about the blowing of the safe in the bank.

"We'll go back to the shaft and get the second sack," said Christian finally.

Gregor nodded. He knew, as he turned up the hill, that he would not get half of what remained of their loot. The generosity of Barry Christian had appeared in the first division of the spoils; now that he had satisfied his superstition, it was unlikely that he would give his companion more than one part in five of what remained. And the great, bright dreams of Gregor grew suddenly dim, and the music of the violins sounded cold and far away.

If he got as much as forty or fifty thousand dollars, he would not blow a penny of it. He would simply buy an annuity. A man was a fool not to make sure of a steady income. What turned a crook into a drunken bum was going broke so often—having to endure frost without a penny in his pockets. Then there was the terror of old age when the prison shakes made it impossible for a man to pick a lock or a pocket. No, every sensible fellow should put aside a nest egg. That was what Duff Gregor would do with his split in this game.

He thought of that as they went up the hill.

Christian, half a step ahead, twice stopped the progress by holding out his hand while he listened.

"What's the matter?" whispered Gregor impatiently.

"There's something in the air," muttered Christian.

"Yeah? You're getting instinctive again," growled Gregor.

They came up to the mouth of the mine, and there Christian waited for as much as five minutes, lying stretched out with his ear to the ground at the entrance to the shaft.

"Listenin' for ghosts?" demanded Gregor.

Christian got to his knees and gave his companion a single silent glance. It was enough to make Gregor decide that he would certainly make no further insolent comments on the state of mind that was now troubling the great criminal. "All right," said Christian calmly. "Give me the lantern. Light that lantern and give it to me."

They had found at the mine a rusted old lantern and a bit of oil in a five-gallon can. They had furbished up the lantern, and now Gregor lighted it and silently handed it to Christian.

"Walk ahead of me," said Barry Christian.

"Hold on!" exclaimed Gregor. "You think that I'd try anything?" "I don't know," said Christian.

He shifted the lantern into his left hand. "Walk ahead of me!" he repeated.

"Barry, what do you mean to do to me in there?"

"Nothing," said Christian, "because I hope that we're going to find the second sack. I hope nothing is going to happen to you!"

"You mean," said Gregor, trembling, "that if we don't find the sack, you'll think I've swiped it?"

"Somebody might have seen us bury the first sack down there by the creek," said Christian, "but nobody could have seen us bury the sack in the mine. Go ahead. Get to the stone and lift it."

Gregor stared, trying to penetrate the mist of brightness that sprang up from the lantern. But all he could see of the face of Christian was as harshly forbidding as a carved stone.

He remembered, then, how many murders had been laid at the door of Barry Christian. Murder of all kinds. He was one who could enjoy the sensations of a gentlemanly duel. Pace off a distance under the eyes of impartial witnesses, turn at a call, shoot. Christian had done that more than once, and always killed his man, though not without collecting some lead in his own person. But he was also ready for other sorts of slaughter. Shooting through a window into a lighted room was something he was not a whit above. Nothing, in fact, that had a practical value to him, would be beneath his pride.

That was the tiger who was to walk behind Gregor into the darkness of the mine. But there was nothing for Duff Gregor to do except shut his teeth so hard together that the shuddering of his jaws ceased. He stepped right into the mine, so briskly that Christian had to caution him to go more slowly.

They came to the first turn on the left and went down the long, ancient shaft. The timbering bulged at the knees. It was green with mold below and cracked with weight above. Water seeped through, here and there. Before their approach, rats squeaked and fled.

Gregor kept drawing in his breath. But there seemed to be no good air, there underground. He could not get enough oxygen. He was stifling.

He found himself standing over the stone. Of course the sack would be under it. And yet—

He laid hold of the edge of the rock, gripped it, and gave a hard pull, for the rock weighed close to two hundred pounds. Up came the stone slab and exposed beneath it a cavity quite large enough to have held the sack—but there was no sign of the treasure.

Duff Gregor knew that death was only a fraction of a second away from him. He sagged forward in the middle of his body, because he expected the bullet to strike him in the middle of the spine.

"Oh, Barry!" he breathed. "You took both sacks, and now you're going to murder me to have me out of the way! Listen to me—"

"You dog, if you could talk like an angel in heaven," said Christian, "I wouldn't listen to you. Gregor, you're a dead man!"

"I want you to listen to me," said Gregor. "I don't care about the money. You can have it. I never expected half of it, and you can have the whole lot, if you want it. I never laid claim to a half of it. You know that. You gave me a half, when I didn't expect it. You know that, Barry. Man, what good'll it do you to murder me? You've got all the money; why d'you want to kill me? I'll never get on your trail, because I know that your kind of medicine is no good for me!"

As he spoke, he knew, before he heard the answer, that he would not win. But the last of his strength of persuasion went into his voice.

Then he heard Christian say: "I'll tell you what I'll do—because you've talked pretty well, and I admire brains in any man. I'll give you your life, Gregor, but you'll have to show me both sacks."

"Don't you think that I'd give you the money if I knew where it was?" cried Gregor.

"No," said the deadly voice of Christian, "because you're a fool and because you think that I won't live up to my promise. You think I'll bargain with you, Gregor. But I tell you I'd rather lose a hundred million dollars than keep my hands off a treacherous cur like you! It's for the good of my own soul that I'm going to kill you!"

"Will you let me turn around and—take it in front?" asked Gregor. "Let me turn around and take it from in front, Barry. For the sake of everything that we've been through together, let me take it from in front. Don't shoot me in the back, like a dog."

"I'm going to shoot you in the back like a dog," said Christian, "because a dog is what you are. It's the only death that's proper for you. Are you ready? Do you want to whine out one prayer before I let you have it?"

A supernatural acuteness came to the ears of Gregor then.

"Look out! They're coming!" he cried.

Christian chuckled. "Are you going to try to make me turn my head with a silly old trick like that?" he asked.

"I hear them!" said Gregor. "I hear—"

And then, quite audibly, a small landslide rattled not far away onto the floor of the shaft. Christian expelled a gasping breath; a gun cracked. The lantern, smashed to bits, was flung to the floor. And then a great voice boomed in the shaft:

"Barry Christian, I've come for you!"

The voice of Christian rose to a scream, not like the scream of a man, but that of a tortured woman.

"Jim Silver!" he yelled.

CHAPTER 25

In the Dark

Gregor had no time to feel thankfulness for his deliverance. He knew, as the lantern was smashed, that Christian had dropped to the floor of the shaft. Gregor did the same thing. He stretched out his hand and touched the foot of Christian—crawling forward to meet the danger.

Gregor himself could not stir at all, for an instant. The thing was not clear in his mind. It seemed like the proceeding of madmen.

Why had they not called on Christian to surrender?

Well, there would have been no sense in that, perhaps. Barry Christian had been in prison before, waiting in the death house for the hangman, and it was said that he preferred death in any form to another spell of waiting in that grim chamber. No, Christian would not surrender. But since that was the case, why had not Silver driven a bullet through his body at once?

Because, perhaps, the prophecy which Christian had made was now about to be fulfilled. One of them was to die neither by knife or gun, but in the bare hands of the other.

Gregor, sick, stifled with fear, gradually forced himself forward. A thin ray of light struck him right in the face. He rolled over to get away from it, and tried a snap shot. Christian, almost beside him, fired at the same time.

The echoes thronged. There was the rattling of another little slide of rocks that had been loosed by the force of the reverberations.

Then the thick, black, damp darkness pressed down on them again. There was such an agony in the spirit of Gregor, such a terrible tenseness of fear, that he thought for a moment that he had been wounded. Only gradually he came to realize that the shuddering contractions of his muscles were not caused by a physical torture.

Out of that desperation came a natural reaction such as occurs in every man of strength and courage, when his back is against the wall. It was impossible that even Jim Silver could readily master the great Barry Christian. And, in the meantime, he, Duff Gregor, might be able to strike some sort of a blow in the dark. No doubt, since Silver was there, Taxi was with him. Well, that would be the meat for Duff Gregor. He knew the size of that slender fellow, and if once he could get his hands on Taxi, he was sure that he could give a quick accounting of him.

He hoped only one thing—that as he groped his way through the darkness, his hands might not encounter a body as large as his own, and enlivened by the spirit of a hunting tiger. He hoped only that he should not encounter Jim Silver, while Taxi fell to the share of Barry.

Gregor forced himself ahead, steadily. If he paused, he knew that the fear would sicken him and make him lie down, shuddering.

The thin ray came again and stabbed him right straight in the face. He wriggled aside from it, and fired instantly. Barry Christian fired, also, and again the echoes in a double roar ran up and down the shaft and knocked several little landslides loose.

How did that devil, hidden in the darkness, know how to find a human face like that with the unshuttered ray of a lantern? How could he feel for and find it?

Then there was a stifled grunt just ahead of him on the right. That was the voice of Christian. The ray of the lantern split the dark again in a single flash, like the stroke of a sword, that cut across the dim picture of two huge men, the force of whose struggles was lifting them from the floor. One was Barry Christian. The other was Jim Silver. It must be he. Taxi was by no means of the same size, and, therefore, Gregor hurled himself forward through the darkness with a savage confidence. If he could beat the small form of Taxi out of his way, if he could dash forward into the open and seize a horse—well, better a life term in a penitentiary than five minutes more of this breathless hell!

So he half rose and dived forward, and a hard, compacted body of a man caught him. The weight of his rush and the superior poundage of his body hurled the smaller figure before him. He yelled with triumph. He lifted the revolver over his head to bring it down on the other. And then the very superiority of his charge brought them both crashing to the ground. An instant later a vice clamped around Gregor's throat. No, he had been caught in the crook of an arm, but it was an arm that knew its business. Red sparks struck across his vision in a whirl.

Well, he would settle the business of Taxi once for all. He twisted his right arm and the revolver in his right hand. And then his right wrist was caught. It was raised, and his hand was beaten down against the floor. The revolver spilled out of the nerveless fingers and rattled far away. Something hard struck big Duff Gregor behind the ear, and there was one red flash in his brain, then darkness.

He knew—sometimes the subconscious mind marks time for us—that his senses were gone hardly half a minute, but when he could see and think again, he was tied. His hands were bound behind his back, and his feet were lashed together. And he heard a panting voice that gasped out: "Keep away from him, Taxi! He's mine. He's all mine!"

Gregor, twisting his head to the side, could see the slender ray of the electric torch cutting again and again across the bodies that were locked together. They were on the floor of the shaft. They twisted this way and that. Then, tumbling once, suddenly they heaved to their feet again. Gregor saw the face of Barry Christian, and closed his eyes to shut out the picture.

While his eyes were dark, Gregor heard the sound of the blow. It was delivered with the fist, he knew. When he looked again, he saw Christian falling. Silver caught him in mid-air, turned him, dropped with him, crushing the inert body under his weight.

"All right," said Silver. "It's over, Taxi."

"He almost got the knife into you, Jim," said Taxi. "Are you hurt, man?"

"Not a scratch," said Silver. "Let's have the light while I tie him."

He tied only the hands of Barry Christian, then he stepped over to Gregor and took him by the hair of his head and jerked the head back.

Gregor could understand. Big Jim Silver's name had been blackened; he had almost lost his life because of Gregor's play acting. And now, shuddering, Gregor waited for blows delivered with the heel of a heavy Colt, blows that would spoil that resemblance between them, blows that would make him a hideous mask forever.

Instead, Silver merely played the light on him for an instant and then said: "I thought it must be you, Gregor."

That was all. But the effect of the words kept reverberating through the mind of Duff Gregor until it seemed that his soul was a mighty chasm, a great emptiness.

He knew then that there would be no personal revenge. There would only be the law. And in spite of himself, no matter how he strained his mind, Gregor could not understand. It was wrong. It was all wrong, he felt.

He heard Christian come to, groaning, and the voice of Silver said: "I wish you'd lasted half a minute longer, Barry. There would never have been a need for a second wait in the death house, then!"

They got out of the mine and to the horses. The prisoners were not lashed hand and foot. Their hands were simply tied behind their backs. Their horses were attached to the horses of their captors, and the first thing that big Duff Gregor noted was the presence of both the canvas sacks.

One thing stuck strongly in Gregor's mind. It was when Silver said: "Look, Taxi. That's the horse that they thought was Parade. That's a bit of an insult, isn't it? Poor old Parade!"

Well, it was in fact an insult, now that the two stallions stood side by side. Gregor could not have said wherein the great dissimilarities lay; he only knew that there was as much difference between the two as there is between painted and real fire.

For that matter, when he felt himself near to the real Jim Silver again, he wondered how even a five-year-old half-wit could have mistaken him for that famous man.

Barry Christian, from that moment, spoke not a word. He kept his head high, and stared at the moon. He looked like a poet drinking in inspiration.

It was Gregor who said: "Well, boys, you got us. But how'd you get at the sacks?"

"The wisest old man in this part of the mountains," said Jim Silver, "told us about every inch of the country for ten miles around, and when he spoke about the old mine, I thought there might be just the ghost of a chance. When we came near enough to spot you, Gregor, we did a little circling about, and it wasn't hard to find your trail down to the creek. I suppose you'd been down there several times a day to take a look at things. I don't blame you, but it left a bit of a trail, and we found it. Afterward, when you went down the hill, we went inside and Taxi's flashlight showed us the way to the rock in the floor of the shaft. It was luck that we lifted it."

"And why," asked Gregor, "didn't you shoot us to bits while we were sitting out in the sun, in front of the mine?"

"Because," said Jim Silver, "in this case it was more important to get the money than it was to get the men. We've had all the luck, though, and corralled you both."

After that, they took the back trail toward far-off Crow's Nest, going down first into the valley. What seemed strange to Duff Gregor was that the two men never congratulated one another on the success of their enterprise. Neither did they speak about any of the joys that they were to encounter in the future, when a shamed community would have to recognize its folly publicly. The trip was made almost entirely in silence, and yet that silence was big, for Gregor, not so much with the knowledge that years of prison life lay ahead of him, but because he was to be the eye-witness to the end of the great Silver-Christian feud, about which men had talked for years.

Well, even in a prison, Duff Gregor would now be a great man. There was no shame in being conquered by Taxi and Silver. Where the great Christian had fallen, he, Duff Gregor, could well afford to fall, also.

They rode out onto the narrow wooden bridge that spanned the river just above the waterfall. On clear, windless days, from the mine, Gregor had been able to hear the murmur of the distant cataract. He heard its more distinct roaring now, sleepily, and the hollow beating of the hoofs of the horses was unreal, like sounds in a dream, also.

Halfway across the bridge, Barry Christian showed what he was made of. He must have spurred his horse deep in both flanks, for the brute leaped suddenly ahead, with a side thrust that almost knocked Parade over the low railing on the opposite side. When that failed, as Silver reached out suddenly for his prisoner, Christian swayed forward, flipped himself out of the saddle, and in falling, struck the rail of the bridge.

The effect was to start his body spinning, and it spun all the way down until it reached the black, swift face of the water beneath.

Gregor, peering over the edge of the bridge, saw the water splash and leap under the impact. Afterward, they could all see the body of the man rise, spinning slowly in the twist of the current.

Taxi drew out a rifle, but Silver held out a forbidding hand.

"The rest has to be outside of our doings," said Silver. "The waterfall will finish Barry Christian."

They saw the body sweep down toward the rocks that fringed the edge of the cataract. "Jim," said Taxi, "there's a chance that he could land on one of those rocks—and get ashore in some way!"

"There's a chance," said Silver. "About one chance in ten thousand. I wouldn't take that chance away from him."

He took off his hat. Taxi turned his quick, nervous glance toward his friend and shook his head.

"The murdering devil," said Taxi. "My hat stays on, no matter how he dies. He ought to have been burned an inch at a time!"

Jim Silver said nothing, and Duff Gregor found himself staring at the big, handsome face of the man he had "doubled"; like a child he was staring and vaguely trying to grasp at the emotions that must be stirring in the great heart of Silver.

CHAPTER 26

The Return

It was early morning when the three rode into Crow's Nest, but men are up early in the West, and the streets were already rather well-filled. They were quickly packed. Before the trio had gone a block, everyone down to the children had poured out of the houses. Even the crowd which had gathered at the house of Henry Wilbur in order to attend the auction, heard the word of what was happening in the main street and came flocking to witness the rare event.

And all was silence as fixed as that which had greeted Silver on his first coming into Crow's Nest.

The explanation was there before their eyes. The "double," who could only exist in fiction, was there before their eyes, riding the horse which was, indeed, a far cry from the greatness of the stallion, Parade.

There was such a crowding, a short distance from the bank, that the riders had to slow up; and then a few questions were fired and answered very briefly but very calmly by Jim Silver. Then the word flew wildly through the town that the night watchman had been no other than the great Barry Christian, and that Christian had been swallowed by the Kendal River, and whirled over the falls just above the town of Kendal.

At last, then, the great trail was ended, and the long and famous duel between Jim Silver and Christian had come to an end. Perhaps that was why the face of Silver was so calm, his eye so unlighted by any malice. No, the explanation seemed to be that the man knew how to forgive. His faint smile was as ready for the citizens of Crow's Nest as, it seemed, for any other men in the world. But to many of the crowd the most interesting figure of the three was Taxi. He was younger than the others, and there was less that was impressive about him. For that very reason, when they measured him with their eyes against their knowledge of what he had done in that very town, he became a hero.

But Crow's Nest was shamed. It was shamed to the heart. That was why there were no more than murmurs, here and there, in the crowd, as room was made for the procession.

It reached the jail, where Sheriff Dick Williams came out into the street and simply threw up his hands at the picture that greeted him. Then, before everyone, he went up to the true Jim Silver and grasped his hand.

"I've been a fool. Forgive me, Silver!" he said.

Silver said, so that a great many people could hear him: "How could you help going wrong, Sheriff? When Barry Christian built a plan, it always seemed as strong as a house. I'm the lucky fellow that I didn't get my neck stretched. I had a lot of luck—and Taxi. That's all that saved me, but I don't blame anyone except a dead man."

Duff Gregor went up the steps of the jail, and at the door he turned and looked down onto the street. It reminded him of the days when he had sat at the entrance to the mine and considered honest men as toiling, stupid ants. Now he saw the toilers thronging about Silver. His last speech had started the shouting. The people waved their hats and yelled themselves hoarse for him, and still they did not know the best part of his story!

Well, there was something in honesty, after all, thought Duff Gregor. As for himself, there was the darkness of prison days. As for Barry Christian, surely there was nothing but the darkness of the grave. But reputation, no matter how evil, had come to

Gregor, increasing his stature. That was why his head was high as he stepped along through the door and heard it clang behind him with a deep and resonant echo that chimed through the steel forest of cells.

Down the street, riding slowly, Silver and Taxi found their way through the crowd, until they came to the bank. There they dismounted and took two big, heavy, well-filled canvas sacks with them into the place. At the entrance, Jim Silver paused and rubbed out with his handkerchief the words which Henry Wilbur had chalked up not long before—that promise to pay with all that he owned in the world.

Silver turned and said to the bystanders: "Somebody please tell Mr. Wilbur that we have found the stolen stuff and it is all here with us. If there's a safe place down here in the bank, he had better come and put it all away."

Happiness makes more noise than anything else. It makes more noise even than hatred.

Because hatred tears the throat with its roaring and is soon forced to silence, but happiness laughs and sings. And all of Crow's Nest was laughing and singing.

That crowd flowed like a river to the Wilbur house. There it gave Henry Wilbur the news. It did more than that. It picked him up on its shoulders and cheered every step of the way that it carried him back to the bank. It picked up Ruth Wilbur, also, and with bad manners and much good nature, it swept her down to the bank, too.

"You saved Jim Silver's neck," they told her, "and Jim Silver saved the neck of Crow's Nest."

They brought her right into the bank; they presented her to Jim Silver with that speech; and then they began to recede, still shouting and roaring and applauding their act.

As the roaring of the crowd withdrew from the big room and beat on the outside of the building like a sea, Henry Wilbur knew that his life work was saved. He knew that his bank had gained fame which was strength that could not fall.

He said: "I want to gather my words, Taxi, so that I can try to thank you. Not to thank you, but to tell you a few of the things that this means. But where's Jim Silver?"

"Hush!" said Taxi. "Don't call him. Don't trouble him. Don't even look at him!"

In spite of that, Wilbur looked, and saw at the rear corner of the big room, half lost behind the forest of bronze-gilt steel bars, big Jim Silver and the girl standing face to face, she with her head thrown back, looking up with something more than a smile on her face.

"What does it mean?" whispered Wilbur.

"Don't ask. Don't think. Hold your breath!" whispered Taxi.

Then they saw Silver bend far over and lift the girl's hand and kiss it. And it did not seem like fancy manners, either.

Also Available

Prologue Books, an imprint of F+W Media, offers readers a vibrant, living record of crime, science fiction, fantasy, and western genres. If you are interested in more classic books that have served as inspiration for contemporary literature, you can discover them today at *www.prologuebooks.com*.